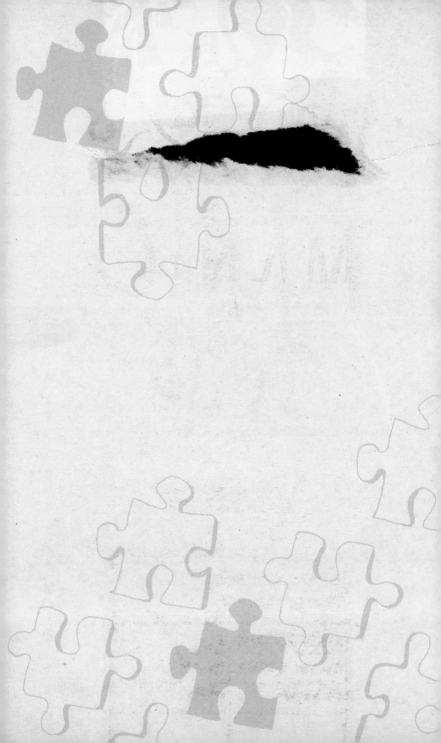

Lilah May's MANIC DAYS

Vanessa Curtis

First published in Great Britain and in the USA in 2012 by
Frances Lincoln Children's Books, 4 Torriano Mews,
Torriano Avenue, London NW5 2RZ
www.franceslincoln.com

A catalogue record for this book is available from the British Library.

ISBN 978-1-84780-246-0

Set in Palatino

Printed and bound by CPI Group (UK) Ltd, Croydon, CR0 4YY in November 2011

1 3 5 7 9 8 6 4 2

To Mum, with love

CHAPTER ONE

'You should ring Bindi, love,' Mum says. 'It's the right thing to do. You two were such good friends!'

I sigh. It's nearly the half-term holiday and I don't know what's right or wrong any more.

I'm not even sure who I am.

It's been a rubbish start to autumn. Mum and Dad are a bit stressed at the moment and, although I know why, it's starting to make me angry. I have a slight problem with anger, you see. It doesn't take much for me to flare up into a rage or to start snapping at Mum or sulking with Dad.

My parents are not, and never have been, exactly 'normal'.

My mother is a clown. Yes, really. She entertains kids at children's parties and she used to be good at it until our family kind of fell to pieces. Then recently

1

she decided to spend more time with me and go to extra yoga classes to keep herself calm, but over the last few weeks I can see that she's getting restless and really wants to go back full-time to her job as a clown.

My dad tames lions and he's quite good at 'taming' *me* when I get angry, but he spends most of his waking hours obsessing about big cats. Sometimes I wish I had a furry mane and a big set of teeth and claws because then he might pay me more attention.

We got a bit hopeful because my brother – Jay – rang up after two years of us not knowing whether he was alive or dead.

I asked him if he forgave me for what I did and the line made this loud humming noise and he wasn't there any more.

We couldn't call him back but the police have been trying to trace the phone box he called from.

Jay still hasn't come home.

And Bindi?

She let me down.

Big time.

Imagine the worst thing that a best friend could do to you, and then triple it. Well, that's what Bindi did to me.

Groo.

✳ ✳ ✳

'Why won't you just ring her up?' Mum says again. 'Friendship is really important, especially at your age.'

We're in the kitchen and Mum has come back from her yoga class and is ready to go to work later. She's standing at the cooker in her clown outfit – today it consists of black-and-white-checked baggy trousers, big, black, lace-up shoes, a frilly white blouse with giant black buttons on and a frizzy red wig which sticks out in tufts on each side.

I glare up from where I've been staring at the television guide for about half an hour. I couldn't actually tell you what's on. All the time I've been staring at the black print there's been a boiling feeling of heat rising up from my feet to my head whenever I think of my so-called best mate Bindi. Even though we've been distracted because of Jay calling, all the time it's been burning away beneath the surface.

I'm fuming.

Maybe I should start keeping my Anger Diary again. I've been *too* angry to write it for the past fortnight.

'Lilah,' my mother is saying. 'Did you hear me? I

3

said you ought to ring Bindi and talk it through with her. She was always such a nice little friend to you.'

I grit my teeth and take a deep breath like Dad has taught me to. I'm supposed to count before speaking in an effort to stop the anger bursting out of my mouth like water from a broken tap.

'Yeah, a nice little boyfriend-stealing friend,' I mutter down at my lap.

Mum hears me and turns around with a fish slice in one hand and the other hand on her hip. It's kind of weird having a clown giving you a serious look. Mum's lipstick is painted on in the shape of a big, red, smiling mouth but her eyes behind the white panda circles look stern and concerned.

'Adam Carter wasn't your boyfriend, Lilah,' she says. 'I think you're being a bit unfair.'

I scrape my chair back and huff off upstairs to my bedroom and slam the door. Then I feel guilty because Mum was making my favourite, fish pie, for dinner and I know she's all worried about losing work during the recession so I creep back downstairs a few minutes later and shuffle sideways back onto my chair in the hope that she won't comment on it.

Benjie turns round three times under my chair, bites the end of his tail and goes to sleep. Sometimes I think that Benjie is my only true friend. Dad got him for me to help with my anger and it's true – I'd never, *ever* take out my anger on this sweet, furry puppy.

Mum spoons out the pie, covers it with peas and we sit at the kitchen table with the lamp on, steam wafting up from our plates and the radio blabbering away in the background.

'Dad's on his way home,' she says. 'Samson hurt his paw.'

Samson is one of my dad's lions at the zoo. Dad says that lions keep him sane – that and going out every Friday for his boys' night out at the pub.

Mum goes to her yoga class every Wednesday evening and comes home all tired and bendy.

And me?

I write in my diary or look at old family photos or listen to Slipknot turned up way too loud.

When I was twelve I used to confide in Jay, until he went all strange and stopped wanting to hang out with his little sister.

After Jay disappeared I talked about my feelings to Bindi.

But that seems a long time ago now.

I know I ought to speak to her but even looking at her makes me feel sick.

There's so much uncertainty lurking about everywhere.

I worry that Jay won't come back.

I worry that I'll hate Bindi forever after what she's done.

I worry that my anger will get out of control again.

'Lilah,' says Mum. She throws our plates into the sink and pulls off her itchy, red wig to rake her fingers through her short, blonde hair. It stands up on end like a demented hedgehog. 'Give Bindi a call. Talk it through. For me?'

She has picked up the phone and is holding it out in my direction.

I take it, grit my teeth and try to calm my pounding heart.

Then I take the phone upstairs, with Mum wishing me luck and making thumbs-up signs in my direction.

I sit on my bed and look at the picture of Bindi and me at last year's school ball.

She's got her arm round my shoulders and we're grinning stupidly. I'm in a blue, strappy, silk dress and she's wearing a gorgeous red sari that her mum made for her.

I look carefully at the photo to see if I can spot anything in Bindi's eyes that might give me a clue as to what happened only a few months after that photo was taken.

I can't see anything there, though, other than friendship and laughter. She just looks the same as always, eyes sparkling and that big, wide grin and perfect white teeth.

I bury my head in the pillow and throw the phone across the room.

CHAPTER TWO

It's getting tough at school.

I used to sit at the back next to Bindi and we'd spend loads of time giggling and passing notes back and forth. Somehow she still managed to get straight As whilst my work went downhill like a mole on a pair of skis, and yet it never made the slightest change to our friendship.

But with Adam Carter it's different.

I've got a thing for him. He's got this cool blonde wing of hair which he gels up into a peak and when he slings a guitar round his neck and stands on stage in his leather biker jacket with a fag (unlit – he actually packed in smoking after I gave him a major lecture about death) hanging from his lip and a bored kind of expression on his face it makes me feel all hot and awestruck by him.

I only once went on a date with Adam and it was a complete and utter *dumptruck*. (That's a Lilah-ism. I have loads of them for different occasions). Anyway, the date sucked. I got angry and climbed up onto a high wall in the cemetery and Adam looked at me as if I were a stranger he didn't want to get to know, and ever since then he's been hanging around more with Bindi than with me.

Groo.

So school is kind of difficult now.

I'm sitting in Chemistry at the back of the class. Bindi's sitting right at the front next to Lola Rodriguez – the class swot. She knows the answers to everything and is another straight-A student, which makes me sick. Adam isn't in my Chemistry class, thank God, or else I would die of embarrassment.

'Right!' barks Mrs Adamson. 'Get into pairs and grab a Bunsen burner, please.'

I see Bindi half turn round and give me a quick look. We used to pair up for everything. Our eyes meet for about a nanosecond and then I grab the arm of Daisy Morrison, the geekiest girl in class, and drag her over to the workspace that runs along the side of the chemistry lab.

'You have to get a Bunsen burner,' says Daisy in her

strange, nasal voice. She blinks at me over the top of thick, black-rimmed glasses. Her hair is tied into two neat blonde plaits by white ribbons with strawberries all over them.

Vile.

'Why can't *you* get it?' I hiss. I run my hand through my own shaggy black hair, making it wilder.

'You're nearer,' says Daisy.

The girl is just *so* annoying. I mean, I'm about two centimetres nearer the equipment cupboard than she is.

'OK, OK,' I mutter. I make for the cupboard and grab a burner from the top shelf, but Bindi's heading there at the same time and we sort of collide in an embarrassing mess of arms and hair and horror.

'Sorry,' she mutters, ducking under my armpit to grab a Bunsen burner and then rushing back to her seat.

I sit down with Daisy and do my best to try and calm down my burning cheeks and thumping heart but it's not easy.

Bumcakes.

Is this what my school life is always going to be like for evermore – me ignoring Bindi and her muttering at me? An endless round of tension and sulking and bad feeling?

As I light the Bunsen burner and watch the blue-orange flame whoosh up into the air I think about what Mum said last night.

Maybe I *should* speak to Bindi properly and try to sort out this mess.

The trouble is, I just hate her so much for having sneaked around with Adam Carter behind my back and if I think about the two of them together it actually makes me retch as if I'm going to be sick.

Daisy's turning down the flame on our burner with a patient sigh.

'You'd have the chemistry lab burned down,' she says.

I glower at her and fiddle with my nose stud. The teachers have given up asking me to remove it because I always put it straight back on about five minutes later.

It's kind of who I am – that angry girl with the nose stud.

I'm not the girl I was three years ago.

It's all because of what happened with Jay.

And now we're waiting – to see if he'll ever come home.

When I get home Mum is sitting on the steps in the hallway with no lights on.

'What is it?' I say, alarmed. She never sits there in the dark. 'Is Dad OK?'

Mum sniffs and flicks the light switch on.

'Yeah, don't worry,' she says. 'He's fine.'

She's wearing normal clothes, which is a bit of a shock because usually when I get home from school she's either just back from a party or is about to go and do one.

I hardly recognise my mother in jeans and a black jumper and boots. She looks young and sad without all the make-up on. Her blonde hair is lank and shapeless and her face is yellow under the harsh light.

I can see all the sadness of the last few years etched into her skin and for a moment I forget about my anger and want to give her a big hug, except I can't, because we've sort of forgotten how to do these things in my family, so we make do with passing head-pats and brief touches on the arm instead.

I place my hand lightly on Mum's shoulder for about three seconds but it's enough to start her off crying again.

I throw my black satchel into the hall and sit down on the step next to her. There's a mirror there so I survey the two of us sitting with our knees hunched up, one of us with dark hair and a scowling expression, the other all tragic and pale and I realise that I almost look older than my mother. I try a smile instead and although my face feels like it might crack I do look a bit more like my real age so I try to hold the smile, but it's no good, the corners of my mouth start trembling so I stop and resume my usual glare.

When Mum has finished crying she blows her nose on a piece of toilet paper and masses of bits of white paper spiral up into the air and then settle like snow on the brown stair-carpet.

'Is it Jay?' I say. It's even hard to mention his name. I never know what reaction I'm going to get.

Mum shakes her head. 'No – well, yes, of course. It's always Jay. But today it's just about me being a useless entertainer.'

I wait. Actually I'm starving and there's no smell of dinner which means we're going to have to wait ages to eat, but I guess I owe it to Mum to listen to her woes, seeing as how she only does all this clown work to be able to help with my school fees.

Mum brushes tissue off her knees and assumes a bright smile. I know it's not real and that she's doing it for my benefit.

'Seems that another mother has complained about me,' she says with a loud sniff. 'She said I didn't look as if my heart was in it any more. Well – I almost asked her if *her* son had gone missing, but I didn't because I'm scared of losing any more clients.'

She hangs her head and starts sniffing again. Oh *raddlewitch*. Visions of mince and potatoes and carrots start to waft past my eyes.

'Tell you what,' I say. 'Why don't we get fish and chips? A surprise for Dad?'

I reckon if I get on my bike and down to the fish and chip shop in five minutes we could be eating in less than half an hour.

Mum nods and gets up. 'Good idea,' she says. 'Sorry, Lilah. I haven't had the energy to cook tonight. I'm a bit worried about all the work I'm losing in this blasted recession.'

I nod but I don't really understand why adults keep wittering on about recession. I mean – we're still going shopping and putting the heating on and booking holidays in this family. So it can't really be all that bad? Right?

Mum is ferreting around in her purse. She hands me a twenty-pound note with another large sigh.

'Go on, then,' she says. 'Plaice for me, haddock

for Dad, whatever you like for you, except a battered sausage.'

My mother has a morbid fear of battered sausages. She says you may as well wrap your heart in lard and then ring for the ambulance.

I get my bike out of the shed and put the lights on before whizzing off into town. The lights in the fish and chip shop are very bright and the hot greasy smell makes my stomach lurch with hunger. The staff are overworked and rushing about shouting orders to the back of the kitchen where a sullen-looking youth in a black-and-white-checked apron is dumping shovel-loads of white frozen chips into hot oil and prodding a few fish about.

I get in the queue and am about to put in my order, so I'm thinking about whether I can afford mushy peas as well as the three fish. Then I get a whiff of something that's so familiar that at first I don't notice it, and then I know at once what it is and my stomach starts to jump with fear, and I turn round as slowly as I can, all the time hoping that it's not who I think it is, and there she is, wrapped up against the cold in a dark wool coat and with a red sparkly Indian scarf around her throat. Of course I knew, because she's always worn this vanilla-smelling 'Soir de Paris' perfume, even though 'Soir de Morley' would be more appropriate, really, since that's where we live.

'Hi Lilah,' she says in a soft, apologetic voice.

'Hi Bindi,' I say in a strangled squawk.

Then I realise that she's not alone and I want the ground to open up and gulp me down quicker than I'm going to gulp this takeaway if I ever get it.

But it doesn't.

'Erm, hi, Lilah,' says the husky deep voice that I know so well.

I lose my appetite.

Just like that.

CHAPTER THREE

Mum finds it hard to believe that it's taken me an hour to pick up three lots of fish and chips from the local takeaway.

She's got a point. I would have only been fifteen minutes, except that after I ran into Bindi and Adam I ordered all the wrong stuff in a moment of insane temper and started coming home with a battered sausage, a saveloy, a chicken and ham pie and three cans of cherry coke. I realised that my parents would go mental so I had to cycle back to the shop, lurk outside until Bindi and Adam had left, go to a cash machine to take out some of my own money and then go in and start ordering haddock and plaice all over again.

I don't explain this, though. Mum'll only have another go at me about not talking to Bindi.

'I'm famished,' says Dad. He flicks the oven on

and starts unwrapping packages and dumping food onto a metal baking tray.

'Oh, you're not going to heat it *up*, are you?' says Mum. 'I'm starving. Let's just eat it.'

They have this argument every time they get fish and chips. Dad is a stickler for things being perfect. Fish and chips have to be heated up on a tray until they're all sizzling and crispy. Mum likes it straight from the paper onto the plate. And I'd eat it on the way home from the shop, given half the chance, except I'm not so hungry now I've seen Bindi, and also it's quite hard to eat fish whilst riding a bike.

'Ten minutes,' says Dad. 'It has to be piping hot.'

Mum makes a face at me behind his back and I give her a smile. It's one of those rare moments where I feel like we're a real family, kind of complete.

Except we're not, of course.

Not until Jay comes home.

* * *

Mum gets more and more depressed about her clown parties over the next few days.

Two more mothers cancel and Mum finds out that a new children's entertainer has set up in business

18

just down the road, so she's moaning to Dad.

'He's got digital equipment, Mark,' she says mournfully. Unusually, all of us are at home for supper at the same time again. 'All I can offer are juggling balls and rabbits coming out of hats. I'm out of date, like a piece of old dried cod.'

As she says this, Dad is sniffing a packet of what looks like out-of-date cod. He lifts the lid of the swingbin and plops it inside.

'I'll pop to the Spar,' he says.

I don't take much notice of any of this.

My head is muddled with thoughts of Bindi and Adam. I keep seeing the way that Adam bends over Bindi, all protective and concerned, and wishing he'd be like that with me instead. But I'm tall and angry and not very cuddly, whereas Bindi is short and sweet and looks like she needs protection.

'Lilah,' Mum is saying. 'Have you done your homework yet? I've got enough problems without the school ringing me up about you. Again.'

The school pretty much have a hotline to this house. I've been in trouble so many times that Mum is now on first-name terms with all the school admin staff and even asks about their babies and stuff on the phone.

'Yeah,' I mutter. Actually I've left my homework and my entire bag at school, what with all the confusing and stressful stuff happening there, but I'm not going to tell her that.

'Do you want to watch your jungle programme then?' she says.

I roll my eyes and sigh.

Mum likes to make out that she only watches these programmes because I enjoy them, but actually it's the other way round. I couldn't give a toss what's happening to Jordan in the celebrity jungle at the moment. My real life is turning into one of those celebrity stories that are splashed across the front of the tabloids every day.

My true love ran off with my only true friend. . .

I shake my head to dismiss all this and head into the lounge behind Mum. She's clutching a huge tub of chocolate ice cream and a large spoon. Comfort eating.

'I need all the help I can get to watch this dreadful programme,' she says, avoiding my eye.

Yeah, right. I know she's addicted to it.

So we're watching the celebrities swallowing nasty bits of kangaroos and wading through swamps full of crocodiles and I'm almost enjoying it, although a bit of me is still seeing Adam and Bindi together, and Dad comes back with some pasta and tomatoes and starts concocting something very garlicky in the kitchen and then the doorbell goes and Mum makes a face at me.

'I hope it's not for me,' she says. 'I need to see whether the camp is going to get dinner tonight or not.'

We're so busy staring at the box that for a minute we think that the shouting noise is something to do with the television and then Mum leaps up and presses the mute button on the remote control and freezes with one hand clutched to her chest.

The shout came from Dad in the hall.

Mum stares at me and I stare back. My heart is pounding with fright. It sounds like Dad is *crying*. Great big choking sobs, as though he's in pain.

'Oh my God,' says Mum. 'What's happened to him?'

She grabs my hand and pulls me out towards the hallway. We're both shaking from head to foot.

It's dark in the hall and there's a smell of burning garlic coming in from the kitchen.

Dad is standing in the hall by the front door in silhouette. At first we can just see him sort of shaking and hear him letting out great barks like a tortured seal or something.

'Mark?' whispers Mum. She feels her way down the hall and flicks the light switch on.

Then she's screaming too and I feel the hair on my arms stand up and my head go dizzy, as if I'm about to pass out.

The air from the open front door rushes down the hall and whips my hair up around my face but I don't notice.

I get there as fast as Mum does and I reach out and do the thing I've wanted to do for over two years.

He says nothing, just lets us.

We stand there in a huddle.

I pinch myself. It's not a dream.

Jay's really here.

CHAPTER FOUR

When things happen that you're not expecting, it's like you're suddenly outside your own body, watching things moving in slow motion.

I can't think of anything at all, but I'm aware of things going on somewhere else in the house – the smell of Dad's dinner burning, the babble of the television, the hum of the washing machine and the lurch as it changes into a spin cycle – but none of it means anything compared to what's just happened to us.

Dad is clearing a path through to the kitchen.

'Let him sit down, let him sit down, Rachel!' he bellows at Mum. 'He's hurt his leg!'

She whimpers but nods.

They brush past me with their arms on either side of him, helping him to walk.

I follow them through into the kitchen with Benjie panting at my heels, trying to moisten my lips with my tongue because my whole mouth has dried to wood chippings.

I hang back, standing by the door and I just stare at him.

My brother.

Real, here, in the flesh, back from wherever he's been for the last two and more years.

Mum rushes to the kettle and fills it up and then she goes to the telephone and rings our GP emergency service.

'My . . . my . . . son,' she starts, but she can't finish the sentence for crying, so Dad takes over.

'No I can't take him into A & E,' he shouts. 'He's in no fit state! I need you round here now.'

Mum makes a hot chocolate with an arm that shakes so hard that the teaspoon clangs against the pottery cup.

'Here . . . here,' she says, putting it in front of him. 'Drink this.'

Jay raises the pottery mug to his mouth and gulps down the contents in about ten seconds flat. Then he

24

brushes his hair out of his eyes and looks around the kitchen at all the things that haven't changed since he last sat in here, and his eyes move right round until finally they fall on me where I'm standing frozen in the doorway.

I can't smile. I want to – that's how I've always imagined this moment would be. In my dreams he comes back and gives me that dazzling smile from underneath his dark floppy hair and he says, 'Hey, Liles,' in his gruff voice and I kind of just know that I'm still special to him, I'm still his little sister and that everything will be OK.

The person looking up at me from the kitchen table isn't my brother.

He's a stranger.

'Lilah,' he manages. 'How old are you now?'

'Fifteen,' I say.

I wasn't even thirteen when Jay left us. It's like a world of difference. Then I was a little girl with long pigtails and a smiley freckled face. Now I'm a whey-faced teenager with dark, shoulder-length hair and a pierced nose and ears. No wonder Jay is looking at me like that.

I guess I'm a stranger too.

A whole load of anger is boiling up in me and that

takes me by surprise.

The last thing I thought would happen when my beloved brother finally came home is that I'd be angry. I thought I'd be too busy feeling love and excitement and relief.

I glance at Mum and Dad. They're white with shock but Mum is crying huge tears of happiness and she can't stop staring at Jay and putting her hand over her mouth and then glancing at Dad.

Benjie has started to bark at Jay now. Of course – he thinks we're being invaded by a stranger. Jay has never seen Benjie before.

Dad takes the puppy into the lounge and shuts him in. Then he leaps into practical mode. That's how he deals with most things. He's acting as if there is a wounded lion on the premises, checking the First Aid kit and trying to find tablets, all the time muttering under his breath. He refills the kettle and makes another round of hot drinks.

'You should drink it too, Lilah,' he says. 'For the shock.'

I take the mug from him but I can't think what to say. I mean, I kind of *am* in shock, even though I hoped and hoped that one day Jay would come home to us. But there's another feeling riding over the top of the shock, and that's the anger.

Questions start to rise up inside me – loads and loads of questions, things that I think we maybe have a right to know, seeing as how we've all gone through hell for the last two years.

I open my mouth to ask one, but Mum has been watching me and she makes a quick despairing gesture with her hands so I close it again.

'Not now,' she says. 'Surely it's enough that he's come home, Lilah?'

I nod, slow and unsure, and take a sip of my hot chocolate.

It should be enough, yeah. But it's not, is it?

There's stuff that needs to be said.

And somehow I know from the burning feelings in my gut that I'm going to be the one who has to say it.

* * *

Dr Woodsman comes round about an hour later carrying his black bag.

'So this is the young man who's caused so much trouble, eh?' he says. Dr Woodsman always speaks exactly like you'd imagine a doctor in a television programme to speak. He looks like one, too, with his grey sideburns, dark eyes and smart suits.

Dr Woodsman has treated Mum and Dad loads more since Jay went missing – Mum for depression and Dad for anxiety – so he knows a fair bit about what Jay's disappearance has done to us as a family.

Jay lets the doctor put his leg up onto a chair and peel back his grimy tracksuit bottoms.

We all let out a sharp breath when he reveals the wound underneath.

'How did you get this?' the doctor asks?

'Dunno,' mutters Jay.

Dad gives him a sharp look.

'Dr Woodsman can't treat you unless you tell him,' he says in his no-nonsense voice.

I wait to see if this voice has any effect at all upon this new stranger Jay.

But it must do, because in a sullen voice Jay says, 'I've been sleeping rough. Got into a fight with one of the other guys. He used a bottle.'

My mother flinches.

'Lilah,' she says. 'Could you go upstairs and put fresh sheets on Jay's bed, please? There are some in the airing cupboard.'

I'm about to start complaining but Dad whirls around and gives me one of his Looks so I back out of the kitchen doorway and stomp upstairs with my thoughts in a mess.

I hear them murmuring in the kitchen for quite a while, all the time I'm unfolding linen sheets and tucking in corners and fluffing up duvets.

When I've finished I take a look around Jay's bedroom.

I've been going in there on my own for two years and wishing more than anything that he was back sitting on that bed playing his guitar and teasing me. I've gone in there and missed him so much that I've cried and picked up the guitars and flicked through all his old music magazines. But now I know that he's about to come up and enter the bedroom I feel really weird, as though I don't want to give up the empty room.

What I had in my head about him coming back is already so different from what's happening downstairs.

I'd kind of forgotten that loads of time apart can make people feel like strangers. And just because you're related to somebody and you've really missed them, doesn't mean that the moment they come through the door it's all smiles and hugs and everything back to how it was before.

I sink down onto the bed and bury my head in my hands.

I feel like the rest of my life has just been cancelled.

This is like a major reality check.

For the first time I realise that Jay being back home might not be all that easy.

I don't like it.

And I don't want him coming up here while I'm still in the room.

What would I say to him?

I leave the room just as he is starting to limp upstairs with Dad supporting him on one side and a brand new bandage pulled tight around his leg.

'Thanks, Lilah,' says Dad as he half-carries Jay back into his old bedroom.

Jay says nothing. He doesn't even look at me.

I guess I don't feature on his radar after whatever has happened to him over the last two years.

Another wave of anger washes over me, sudden, red and hot.

'Bed, Lilah!' Mum calls up the stairs. Her voice is cracked with weariness and emotion.

I go into my room without having to be asked twice.

I stare at the photo of Jay on the white dressing

table, next to the old photo of me and Bindi when we were ten.

Then I bury my face in my oldest teddy-bear and let out a silent scream until I'm choking on fake fur and dust and have to come up for air.

The next day, the next few days, the next few months, years and the rest of my life lie ahead of me now, alien and strange and without the usual comforting rituals of me, Mum and Dad.

It's all going to be different.

'I don't ever want to get up again,' I mutter to the bear.

Then I get into bed and stare at the ceiling for hours.

CHAPTER FIVE

When I wake up the next morning after about two hours sleep I lie in bed with Benjie weighing my feet down, listening to the house coming alive, just like I do every morning.

There's the dull whoosh and hum of the boiler waking up downstairs and then the steady drone of my bedroom radiator coming on.

There's the creak of floorboards in Mum and Dad's room, the sound of their door opening and Dad going into the bathroom and locking the door.

There's the gentle tread of Mum on the stairs as she goes down to make tea for her and Dad and the hiss of water being poured into the kettle, the click of the switch.

I wait.

She makes tea and comes upstairs again just as Dad comes out of the bathroom.

Then there's silence.

That makes me sit up, straining my ears.

Usually they start to laugh about something or have a vague argument. Over the last few months Mum finally got her giggle back again after it having gone on holiday for over two years.

I try to hear something, anything, but I can only make out the quietest murmur of voices behind their closed door.

Great.

Things have changed already. Jay has only been home for about ten hours and already the house feels different – colder, more uncertain.

It's Saturday, which means I don't have the excuse of rushing off to school, either.

Not that I really want to go there, what with Bindi and Adam and all of that, but at least I could hook up with some of the other girls and have a bit of a gossip about who's been booted out of the celebrity jungle or who's reading the latest Twilight novel.

Normal stuff.

Something tells me that today isn't going to be very normal.

I turf Benjie off my feet, get out of bed, put on my thick pink dressing gown and run a brush through my tangled black hair.

I shuffle downstairs in my slippers, coughing. The kettle should still be hot.

As I pass Jay's door I try to walk really quietly. I don't want him to wake up. Ever. If that sounds mean, it's not supposed to. It's just that I don't know what to say.

I don't know what to say to my brother after two long years of waiting for him to come home again.

I make it to the kitchen and drop a teabag into a cup and drink the tea staring out at the yellow leaves scattered all over the muddy lawn. A robin is sitting on top of the handle of Dad's spade. It looks at me sideways out of one eye, as if it knows my thoughts. Against the fading green of the garden its breast looks really bright red, like lipstick or blood.

I'm still standing there lost in thought, swaying slightly to keep warm, when Mum creeps downstairs again and comes to join me.

She looks really pale, as though she hasn't slept, and there are purple shadows underneath her eyes. And not from clown make-up, either.

'Rough night,' she offers, making up a cafetière

of coffee and pouring herself a steaming cup of hot black liquid. 'Too much to think about.'

I nod.

For some reason neither of us can actually mention Jay. It's like when he was missing and I didn't dare mention his name in case it started Mum crying or Dad shouting. But it's different now. I don't think Mum would cry if I said his name. I think she'd look at me with big scared eyes and maybe admit that she didn't know what the hell to do next, just like me.

I try it out to see if my theory is right.

'Is Jay going to come down for breakfast, do you think?' I say.

Mum stares out at the garden for a moment, as if she's looking to the robin for an answer.

I bet that robin wishes he hadn't landed in our garden this morning. Too much stress for a little feathered thing.

Mum turns to look at me. Her eyes are frightened, just as I predicted. Her mouth is smiling, though – or trying to.

'I don't know, love,' she says. 'We mustn't push him on his first day back. He's been through so much.'

'We *all* have,' I mutter.

She pretends not to hear me and starts messing

around getting eggs and bacon out of the fridge. When she turns around again her voice is calm and careful.

'And now he's back,' she says. 'This is the best present we ever could have wished for. So you're not to go upsetting him, OK?'

I brush past her and storm upstairs.

Me upsetting *him*? What about the two years of upset he's caused to *us*? All the crying and screaming and arguments and bad times at school and the anger that consumed me for all that time and still seems not to be letting up much now.

As I go past his door I do what I used to do in the early days after he disappeared.

I give it a good swift hard kick. I don't care about waking him up now.

Groo.

I forgot I was wearing slippers.

I hop into my bedroom and lie on the bed in agony and then the bad night catches up with me and I start falling asleep.

The next thing I know it's three hours later and when I stagger back into the hallway Jay's bedroom door is open and the curtains thrown back.

I go back downstairs and there are the remains of

breakfast on the table but Jay's nowhere to be seen.

'He's gone with Mum to the chemist to get some more bandages and stuff,' says Dad. He looks white around the eyes and he's moving very slowly, like a lion that's been shot in the leg with a dart and might collapse at any moment. 'Sit down and I'll get you some breakfast.'

I sit at the table and push the dirty plates away.

'It's not a hotel,' snaps Dad. 'You could put them in the sink if they bother you that much.'

Great. So now Dad is having a go at me too.

But even as tears well up in my eyes I can see that he's not really cross with me. He's feeling as though he can't control the situation. Dad's brilliant around lions because he knows exactly how to handle them. If they roar, he calms them down. If they play, he joins in. If they're hurt, he gets the vet in to sort them out.

It's hard to believe that a big man like my dad could feel uncertain or unsure about anything.

That makes me more scared than anything.

Dad doesn't know how to handle his own son.

So how will I cope with having my brother back?

CHAPTER SIX

LILAH'S ANGER DIARY   OCTOBER 12TH, 4.00 P.M.
ANGER LEVELS: 8/10

I haven't written in my Anger Diary properly for over two months. Last time I wrote was to say that things were getting better with Mum and Dad and that somehow we've managed to become a family unit again, even without Jay. Ha! That's a bit rubbish now, isn't it?

It's weird – I'd actually stopped being angry about Jay, at last, and Dad hadn't had to have one of his Taming Lilah sessions for ages, even though the situation with Bindi and Adam has been rumbling on underneath all this time and I have to take deep calming breaths like Dad showed me last year. I'm more just sick and tired of it these days.

But now Jay is home and I feel the exact opposite of how

I always thought I would do when he finally came through that front door. I thought it would be like the missing piece of a jigsaw puzzle being plopped into place and completing the picture of blue sky and yellow sun and a peaceful scene on a river with boats going up and down and red buses trundling by on the road. But I didn't reckon on the rest of the jigsaw puzzle having gone a bit warped and mouldy over the last two years and the other pieces all having changed in shape and size and colour. That's me, Mum and Dad, see? We're the rest of the puzzle. And we've changed over the last two years. A lot. We've had to. And the missing piece doesn't really fit any more.

Jay's been home for nearly a week now.

He's spent most of his time shut upstairs in his bedroom muttering into his mobile phone. Mum had to buy him a new phone and I can see she wasn't exactly happy about encouraging him to spend yet more time closeted away in private speaking to people she doesn't know, but he got so agitated about not having a phone that she caved in.

Jay and I haven't exchanged more than about three words. If I see him coming downstairs I usually rush out the front door and go down to the precinct. If I hear him coming upstairs I put music on and shut my door.

The only time we all sit together as a family is at breakfast and I bolt my cereal as fast as possible so that I can take Benjie for his walk in the park if it's a weekend or else get off to school for another depressing day of watching Bindi and Adam whispering together at break time and wandering about school together, lost in their own little world.

Mum's finally got Jay to have a bath. He smelled so bad that I sometimes thought I was going to faint when I was in the same room.

'Lilah, he *has* been living on the streets for two years,' whispers Mum to me. 'What did you think he was going to smell like? Roses and fabric conditioner?'

Mum has got very sarcastic over the last week. I think it's her way of coping with Jay being back. She's put all her clown commissions on hold and got her deputy to do the parties so that she can concentrate on trying to make Jay feel at home again. She spent about three hundred pounds at the supermarket buying all his favourite foods and loads of stuff to 'build him up' because he's come home even skinnier than he was when he left two years ago.

Dad is still working at Morley Zoo but he gets home earlier than usual and attempts to have 'man to man' conversations with Jay at the kitchen table.

I don't think that this is working.

Sometimes I creep downstairs when they're having one of their 'chats' and I sit on the bottom step in the hall in the dark, hug my knees to my chest and listen.

Jay just sits with his head bowed, fiddling with the black leather bands on his skinny wrist and dipping his long dirty-brown hair down over his face so that Dad can't see what he's thinking.

'So how about we go to a game on Saturday?' Dad says. He's always suggesting things like this now. I don't know why – Jay never liked football in the first place. The only thing that he was passionate about was music. And now he never listens to that, either.

Dad gets fed up of asking questions that don't receive answers after a while and wanders outside to sow some seeds for winter vegetables. I scurry back upstairs again so that Jay can't see me.

It's the half-term holidays in a week. I'm dreading them.

Groo.

There won't be school to escape to, the weather will probably be bad and I've got two weeks stuck in the house with a brother I can't talk to any more and two stressed-out, edgy and desperate parents who have forgotten that I exist.

Oh, and an ex-best-friend who is expecting the baby of my favourite ever boy. Did I mention that bit? Yeah – Bindi's got herself pregnant. By Adam, my one true love.

Bombutts!

At this rate, Dad might have to start taming me again.

CHAPTER SEVEN

The last week before half-term is rubbish.

We get one day when we can wear our own clothes so I go all-out to express how I'm feeling inside. Bindi comes in wearing one of her beautiful pink silk saris, with a gold ring through her nose and a little red dot on her forehead, and I am guessing that Adam's dribbling with admiration for her. It makes me feel sick so I try not to look, but it's hard. Adam's wearing a white T-shirt and black jeans and black converse trainers and he's gelled his blonde hair up a bit so that he looks exactly like a rock star. They make a weird couple, Bindi all shy and girly and feminine and Adam all sharp angles and tight clothes, but somehow it kind of works and I have to admit that they look good together.

Groo.

This is what I wear to own-clothes day:

Black biker jacket.

Stud in my nose.

Black and white striped top.

Ripped black jeans.

Black studded biker boots.

I can see Miss Gorman nearly having a heart attack when she sees all my piercings, but as it's the only day when teachers are not allowed to tell us off about clothing and jewellery, she clamps her lips together and gives me a tight little smile with about as much warmth as an icicle in it and then passes by.

We don't have many lessons as it's the last day before the holidays and then we all pile into the canteen for the usual Jamie Oliver healthy-style lunch but there's a buzz in the air, anyway. I'm chatting in a vague fashion to Amelie Warner, who was my enemy last year, but we've forgotten about all that and she's giving me advice on lip glosses and I'm trying to look interested, and then I catch something weird out of the corner of my eye.

Adam Carter is looking at me.

Only because he thinks I can't see.

But I can.

Bindi is sitting next to him and she catches him

looking over and her bright smile fades just a little bit and she makes a big thing out of reaching over him to get at the water jug so that he turns away again.

But I saw it.

He was looking at me.

For the rest of the afternoon I can't concentrate on anything at all, even though we're supposed to be tidying out our lockers and sweeping up the art room. I keep expecting him to look at me again, but he never does.

As everyone heads for the gates at three I see him and Bindi heading off towards a big blue Range Rover where Mrs Carter is waiting to take her son home.

'Bye,' I say in a small quiet voice to myself. 'Have fun.'

Then I drag my feet towards home and the bleak atmosphere that lives inside it.

***

When I get home there's a weird woman sitting at the kitchen table with Mum and Jay. Dad's there too, which is unusual as he's normally not at home this early.

As soon as I see this I make to head up the stairs

and hide away in the nice dark mess of my room, but Mum comes into the hall and grabs my arm.

'Oh no you don't,' she says. 'Come in here. We need to talk to you too.'

I can see how the children at Mum's parties could be frightened of her. Even without the scary clown outfit she has a ring of steel to her voice. I roll my eyes but she's obviously not in the mood for argument so I slope into the kitchen, offer a faint grunt and slump at the table.

'This is Dr Cunningham,' says Mum. 'Dr Woodsman has referred us to her. She's a . . . what did you say you were?'

The woman smiles. She's left a rim of pale pink lipstick all round the edge of Mum's white flower mug.

'I'm a psychologist,' she says, 'specialising in teenage behavioural issues and family therapy.'

For some reason I feel like shrivelling up into a little ball and rolling underneath the kitchen door into the hallway when she says that. The woman is observing me with a calm smile. Her eyes seem to bore through my face, into my brain and right down to my soul where all my anger lies waiting for the next opportunity to burst out.

'Hello, Lilah,' she says. 'I've heard lots about you.'

'Great,' I mutter. 'I've actually got a lot of homework to do.'

Mum and Dad both give a big snort at that. Only Jay doesn't react. He's staring down at his lap and I notice that his hands are shaking on the table.

In the old days he'd have caught my eye and smiled and we'd have been plunged into that deep, comforting world where we lived together and ganged up against the Old Dudes.

'It's the half-term holidays, Lilah,' says Dad. 'Don't be ridiculous. You don't have much homework, surely?'

I mumble something about an exam in November but it's no good. They're on to me.

'You don't have exams in November,' says Dad.

'Dr Cunningham has come to help Jay get used to being at home again,' says Mum. 'And that affects all of us. So you're jolly well going to take part. OK?'

'OK,' I say. Inside I feel sick. Some holiday this is going to be.

Mum takes us all into the lounge where it's warmer because Dad has put on the gas fire and arranged some chairs around in a circle. Our lounge looks like a waiting room in a doctor's surgery.

I glance at Jay. He's looking even more pissed off than I feel. I keep looking, willing him to catch my eye like he used to do, waiting for some little sign that this terrible barrier between us is going to start crumbling down.

Nothing. He doesn't even seem to register that I'm in the room.

Mum and Dad sit down and gesture for us to follow. Dr Cunningham sits in the middle with a notepad on her knee.

I see Dad giving her admiring glances when he thinks Mum isn't looking. He has forgotten that women have a special radar that means that they can see out of the front, side and back of their head without seeming to move their eyes.

Dr Cunningham is wearing a tight pencil skirt and a glamorous mock-fur wrap. She also has those mad-scientist black glasses on and has fair hair caught in a clip at the back of her head. The only thing that lets the look down is her shoes. They are plain black loafers with no style whatsoever. I suppose she can't wear silly fashion shoes when she's going round to people's houses and dealing with the unknown. Maybe she needs to be able to leg it fast if a client turns out to be a nutter.

I'm so busy starting at Dr Cunningham's horrible shoes that I don't notice she's addressing a sentence to me until Mum gives me a furious nudge with her elbow and snaps, 'Lilah!' with a cross look on her face.

'Sorry, what?' I mutter.

'That's all right,' smiles Dr Cunningham. 'I was just asking you, Lilah, if you could put into words your feelings about Jay coming home again?'

Groo.

Like I can just come out with all that! I can't even find the right words to put it down in my secret diary, let alone blather it out to four watchful faces. Well, three, because Jay is still staring down at his feet with his hair hanging right over his pale face.

'Erm,' I start. I look over at Dad for encouragement. He gives me a wink and leans forwards with his elbows on his knees, eyes lit up with determination.

'Go on, Lilah,' he says. 'Nobody's going to get angry if you say how you feel.'

Except me.

I'm worried – worried that if I start expressing my innermost feelings I'll get that familiar rise of hot anger spreading up from my feet through my chest and out of my mouth into a spew of horrible words.

But Dad looks so anxious and he's obviously willing me to start speaking, so I clear my throat without looking at Jay and I say, 'I spent two years wishing he would come back. I wished it every day, even though just before he left he was acting like an idiot. And now he's back it's like some stranger is living in our house. And he won't even look at me. And even if he did, I'm not sure I know who he is.'

There's a short silence when I stop speaking. I glance at Mum. She's trying not to cry. Dad is nodding at me.

'That's very honest, Lilah,' says Dr Cunningham. 'Well done for that. It can't have been easy to say it.'

She turns towards Jay who hasn't moved even an inch since I came into the room.

'And now perhaps you'd like to say something back to your sister?' she says. 'Anything? First thing that comes into your head?'

There's a sort of heightened hush, like you get at a concert when the orchestra are about to put their bows on their instruments and the conductor has his arms raised ready to bring down his baton and the audience are holding their breaths for that first, powerful sound.

Except that Jay doesn't say anything.

He sits for a few more seconds and then stands up so fast that the chair nearly tips over backwards. He leaves the room almost without sound, as though his feet were made of feathers, even though our floor is hard and wooden and most people sound like elephants on it. There's the faint slam of his bedroom door shutting upstairs and then silence.

Jay only listens to his music on headphones now.

Sometimes he doesn't listen to it at all.

I mention this to Dr Cunningham as nobody's saying anything and it's all getting a bit awkward.

'That's quite normal,' she says. 'Music can be very emotive. Jay probably doesn't want to risk re-living all his memories of the time before he ran away. Music can bring lots of feelings back that people often want to shut away.'

It makes sense so I nod and sit back in my chair. She's good.

After that Dr Cunningham talks to Mum and Dad and I settle back and almost fall asleep with the warmth of the fire and their murmuring voices, except I'm looking at them all as they're talking and I'm comparing Dr Cunningham's glamorous lipsticked face and smart clothes to Mum's worn-down, stained tracksuit bottoms and her haggard, creased face.

I almost miss her clown look. Mum hasn't been to work since Jay got home. I forgot that underneath her clown make-up she's got real wrinkles and shadows under her eyes from month after month of broken nights.

After Dr Cunningham has left, I go up to Mum and do something I haven't done for about three years.

I put my arms around her and bury my head in her chest.

Mum is so surprised that she stands frozen still for a moment with her arms by her sides. Then she hugs me back and cries a bit and then we both laugh.

'Women!' says Dad. But he's smiling.

He heads off into the kitchen and puts a frozen lasagne in the oven for supper.

Jay comes down for the meal and eats it as if it is the last meal available in the world ever.

He doesn't speak, though – just shovels in the food with a fork and no knife.

He leaves the table before pudding and goes back upstairs so we all just carry on eating lemon meringue pie, which makes me feel sick, but I'm too worn out to argue so I'm swallowing the slimy yellow lumps and sugary chewy topping and trying to look as if I am enjoying it when Mum freezes for the second time that night.

'Where's he going?' she whispers. All the colour has drained from her already-pale cheeks so that she looks almost see-through.

We stop talking. The front door clicks shut.

Dad gets up and runs into the lounge to peer out of the window.

'He's going down towards the precinct,' he says. 'Don't worry, Rachel. He's probably gone to get cigarettes.'

Mum is gripping on to the edge of the kitchen table as if she's going to fall. Dad tops up her wine and rubs her arm.

'He'll be back later,' he says. 'Honest. Why would he have come home just to run away again? It doesn't make sense. Eat your pudding.'

We try to carry on as if nothing has happened but none of us can think of a thing to say.

There are a lot of clinking noises as our spoons hit the empty bowls and Mum gathers up the dishes and plonks them into the sink.

I go to bed at eleven and Dad goes up to his study just afterwards.

Jay still doesn't come back.

CHAPTER EIGHT

I've left a gap again. Sorry. So Jay did come back just before midnight on that evening. But by then I'd got so angry I had to come upstairs and knock my head against the wall about one hundred times. Dad was listening to music in his study so he didn't hear me, thank God. I could so do without Dad trying to 'tame' me at the moment. And Mum was too busy waiting and watching the clock to notice that I was nearly knocking myself out on the cold white Artex of my bedroom wall.

I hate Jay – really hate him. How could he go out and put us through another night of that horrid worry all over again? After we had to go through over two years of hell, wondering where he was and whether we'd ever see him again. I hate him.

No I don't. Well – I do today. Maybe I'll get over it. Dunno. I'm so angry at the moment that I can't even bear to be in the same room as him. We've got into this pattern of mostly ignoring each other.

I'm back at school, Bindi and Adam are still going around together and it's getting really cold. Groo.

(A bit later: I shouldn't write that I hate Jay. Feel bad about writing that now. I know I don't exactly hate him. But I don't love him much at the moment, either).

***

Mum drags me out at the weekend to do some early Christmas shopping. None of us have given it much thought what with Jay coming back out of the blue, but now she seems dead keen to fill a huge trolley with mince pies and puddings and a big frozen turkey. She adds two boxes of coloured shiny crackers and one of party poppers.

'Steady on, Mum,' I say. 'Are you sure Jay's going to be in the mood for party poppers?'

Mum is unloading all this food onto the conveyor belt with a purposeful glint in her eye.

'Well, even if he isn't, *we* are going to have the best Christmas ever,' she says. 'I've had two Christmases without my son. And now he's back. Get me a box of After Eights from over there, Lilah, will you?'

I sigh and head off to the chocolate section.

Something tells me that this Christmas is in some ways going to be even worse than the two we had without Jay. How are we going to do 'Happy Christmas' when one member of the family won't even speak and sucks up all the positive energy in the room until it turns black and foul, almost as though you could reach out and wring a dark, dank liquid out of it?

Mum loads all our bags into the car and then drags me off to River Island. I kind of like going in there on my own on Saturday mornings but going in there with my mother in the middle of the Christmas rush is a mega nightmare. And she doesn't want to look at all the good stuff, like the hooped earrings and black leather studded pumps; she wants to drag me into the boys' section to choose something for Jay.

'I'm not sure he's into clothes at the moment,' I say. Jay has been wearing the same stained top and old jeans for the last week.

'Well, we can't give him anything to do with music,' says Mum. 'Dr Cunningham thinks it might awaken painful memories and that we should let him choose when he's ready to play the guitar again.'

'OK,' I say. I know when I'm beaten. It's hot in here and people are starting to get bad-tempered in the queue, muttering about there not being enough staff on.

Mum settles on a striped, long-sleeved top, a bit like one I've already got. She buys a big black jumper and a pair of black jeans. I have to admit that she's got good taste and that the Jay from our previous life might have liked these things.

'Right,' she says. 'And now your father.'

My heart sinks down into my black Uggs and dies. This can only mean one thing. Department Store Hell.

By the time we've fought our way around an enormous store full of the stench of perfume testers and crowded with anxious shoppers filling their trolleys with more Christmas rubbish, I've almost lost the will to live.

'Seagullvians,' I mutter as a group of people with sharp elbows push past me and nearly knock me flying.

'What?' says Mum, but she's not really listening. She's got her eye on a V-necked jumper for Dad and starts rifling through a stack of different sizes. Mum has got so used to my 'Lilah-isms' that she doesn't really hear them any longer.

I hop from one leg to another to try and stop from screaming as Mum pulls out one jumper after another and then stares at them and puts them back, muttering about sizes to herself.

'And what about you?' she says when we've finally paid for the jumper and I've burst into the fresh air outside with relief. 'What would you like for Christmas, Lilah? We could go and choose it now if you like.'

I turn away from Mum and face an enormous wave of shoppers who are coming towards me with their eyes fixed on the door of the department store.

There are tears springing up in my eyes. I don't want her to see because she's trying to be really nice and is buying everyone expensive presents.

The thing is there *is* something I would like for Christmas, only you can't buy it in a shop. And just thinking about it is making me turn into an emotional wreck.

'A black top would be nice,' I manage to squeak out in the frosty air.

Mum looks pleased. 'Topshop?' she says. The woman has boundless energy for shopping.

I stagger along behind her. How can I tell Mum that the only thing I want for Christmas, she can't provide?

I go into the changing rooms with Mum and try on some tops and they look nice so we choose a black stretchy one together and she's happy about that but all the time I'm fighting down this great wave of sadness and all I can think as we head back to the car park and nearly get into a punch-up with another car that tries to get into our space before we've left it is one thing.

I want my brother back. Again.

The following weekend I wake up to a world of white outside the window.

It's perfect.

The snow looks unbroken and fresh on our back lawn, except for a tiny line of cat footprints left by the chocolate Siamese kitten from next door.

Our street is dead quiet except for the occasional car grinding its way slowly down the road at about ten miles an hour. I watch out of the lounge window as people walk past in wellington and Ugg boots, placing one foot in front of another with great care.

'Brrr!' says Mum, clicking the thermostat up in the kitchen. 'Don't tell me we're actually going to have a white Christmas! I hope Dad doesn't get snowed in at the zoo!'

She cooks up some scrambled eggs on brown toast and as there's no sound from Jay's bedroom we eat it together in companionable silence, perched on the windowsill and staring at the unfamiliar landscape outside.

'You and Jay made a wonderful snowman when you were about ten,' Mum says, out of the blue. 'You used chocolate buttons for his eyes and a parsnip for his nose. Took you all morning to finish.'

She wipes her eyes on the red cord sleeve of her dressing gown and stares out at the whiteness for a moment or two longer without speaking.

I feel like something is about to burst out of me. I'm not sure what it is. It's not my usual anger. It's not exactly sadness, either. No – it's more a sense of growing excitement. And determination. And like there's an invisible string linking me back to the past, when Jay and I built the snowman.

Why shouldn't things be that good again?

'Wait there,' I say to Mum.

I pull on my thickest black winter coat, a stripy scarf and woolly gloves and I pound out onto the powdery snow in the front garden. The crispness of the air threatens to suck my breath away and my feet get wet even through my black biker boots, but I don't care.

Mum laughs at me through the window as I dart this way and that, piling up snow into head and stomach-shaped balls and patting the sides to make them rounder. By the time I've finished my cheeks are flushed and numb with cold and my nose is dripping but I don't care. I run inside, grab a carrot and two coins and give the snowman a face. Then I get one of Dad's old baseball caps and stick it on top. I stand back to admire my work.

Not bad.

Mum is clapping through the window. I haven't seen her smile like that for ages.

Since Jay got back, in fact.

I glance up at Jay's bedroom windows – curtains pulled tight across like he doesn't want the outside world to ever get in. It will be like a sealed tomb in there. Jay hates fresh air and light.

I pick up a handful of snow and I lob it up at his window – hard.

The snowball shatters and showers me with cold wet ice but I remould another one and throw again, and again, until the curtains part about an inch and Jay's cross face peers out and then looks down at me.

I chuck another snowball, making him jump back as it hits the glass where he's pressed his nose.

'Hey!' I yell. 'Get down here and help me with this snowman, will you?'

The curtains are redrawn.

Silence.

I become aware of how cold and wet I am and I pull my sleeves down as far as they can go and huddle by my snowman.

I wait.

And I wait.

Nothing.

The sky looks grey and unfriendly and I'm just thinking of going in to soak in a nice hot bath when the front door creaks open and Jay comes out into the snow, wearing a coat over his pyjamas and wellington boots underneath.

'Christ, Liles,' is all he says, but it's enough.

It's the first time he's used my nickname since he got back. It's the first time he's *spoken* to me since that first evening.

He goes over and surveys my snowman and then with a sudden spurt of energy he rebuilds the entire thing and adds stumpy legs and arms and a branch sticking out of its mouth as though it's smoking a cigarette.

I stand back and I watch my big brother mould the snow and I don't say anything, but inside I'm holding my breath in case this is a dream and I'm going to wake up or in case I say the wrong thing and shatter this moment.

'That's better,' says Jay. He stamps his snowy boots on the front doorstep and goes back inside and up to his room.

I stand there all stunned for a moment. The snowman stares back at me with his flat copper eyes.

The curtain in the front lounge moves a little and I see Mum's face emerge from behind it. She's been watching us all the while.

I give her a small cautious smile and she returns it.

Then I brush the snow off my coat and head back inside.

* * *

Jay spends the rest of that day back up in his bedroom.

I'm kind of disappointed. I thought perhaps he might come down and chat to us a bit, but there's no sound from upstairs, and by the time Dad comes home from Morley Zoo we've given up expecting him to surface and I'm helping Mum make supper in the kitchen.

'Don't expect miracles, Lilah,' Mum says to me as I peel potatoes and chop up a pile of French beans. 'That must have been a big effort for him, coming outside to help you.'

I nod. I know that, deep down. But I just want everything to be back to normal so that we can have a family Christmas like the ones we used to have.

'We'll still have a good Christmas,' says Mum, doing that spooky mind-reading thing that mothers do. 'At least this year we won't be worrying about where Jay is!'

I think back to the last two Christmas days in the May household. Mum crying as she cooks the turkey. Dad trying too hard to be jolly and then ending up rowing with Mum because she can't do the same. The empty chair at the dining-table. The lack of games because Jay had been the great one at making them up and having us all in fits of laughter. The staring at the television while each of us had our own private thoughts. The early nights and the relief when the whole Christmas holiday was over.

'Yeah,' I say. 'Yeah. It should be better than last year.'

Dad comes home with snow on his clothes from being outside in the lion enclosures all day.

'Shakira's trying to eat her babies,' he says in a mournful voice. 'We had to take them away from her. You should have heard her roaring.'

Mum sighs. She goes upstairs with a tray and puts it outside Jay's bedroom and then she comes back down and plonks a plate of shepherd's pie in front of Dad. She's heard these stories over and over during the last ten years.

Dad gulps red wine and eats dinner with enthusiasm. Mum and I pick at the potato topping and mess about with the mince. She looks at me and raises her eyebrows.

'Oh,' I say, after I realise what she's trying to do. 'Yes. Erm, Dad. Jay came down and made a snowman with me.'

Dad puts his knife and fork down at that.

'Really?' he says. 'That's brilliant. Did he talk to you, Lilah?'

'Two words,' I say. 'But I guess that's an improvement on nothing.'

'It is indeed,' says Dad. 'I think this calls for more wine.' He pours me some even though I don't really like it, and tops up Mum's glass.

'Maybe after Christmas you could think about going back to work?' he says to Mum. 'You must be missing it, Rachel.'

Mum gives him one of her Looks.

'Firstly,' she says. 'I don't miss being pelted with food by badly-behaved seven year olds. I don't miss having to wear a hideous clown outfit and an itchy wig and painting my skin with so much crap that it has broken out in protest. And secondly, my son needs me.'

'Not to mention your daughter,' I mutter but she glares at me.

'You get plenty of attention,' Mum snaps. 'Don't be so selfish. Your brother has been through hell out there on the streets for two years.'

I stand up and head for the door. It's either that, or feel the familiar old prickles of anger start up again. If

66

I stay I'll just start shouting about the hell that we've *all* had to go through over the last two years and I'll end up having Mum in tears and Dad slamming up to his study and I don't want to ruin the rest of the evening after Jay spoke those two precious words to me in the morning so I go upstairs and lie on my bed and try not to cry instead.

I'm still lying there at half past ten wondering if I've got the energy to get ready for bed and then my mobile rings which is unusual because the person who used to ring it most was Bindi, and of course we're not talking, so it can't be her.

I pick up the phone and nearly die of shock. The display is flashing 'Adam' at me.

Adam Carter! What on earth does *he* want?

He's got some nerve, ringing me up.

But as ever I'm too nosy to ignore it, so I press the green button and make my voice as cool as I can.

'Hey Adam,' I say. 'What's up?'

CHAPTER NINE

There's a silence after I say that.

I can almost see Adam pacing up and down in his bedroom. He'll be running his hands through his blonde hair and preparing to speak in a very low voice so that his mother doesn't overhear.

He's got music on in the background – Black Eyed Peas, by the sound of it. He likes Songs With Attitude. Sadly he doesn't like Girls With Attitude. This is why he's going out with Bindi and not with me. Bindi hasn't got any attitude at all. When she walks into a room full of people she kind of melts into the crowd without anybody much noticing. When I walk into a room people turn round and give me looks of suspicion. That's because I always look as though I'm angling for a fight, at least according to Dad.

'You've got such an angelic face, Lilah,' he says. 'Shame you have to scowl all the time and ruin it.'

I'm scowling now. Just the effort of hanging on to the mobile with Adam breathing on the other end of it is making me feel angry again.

Benjie pokes his nose around the door and bounds towards me so I scoop him up under one arm and sit down on the bed.

'What do you want, Adam?' I say. 'I'm kind of in the middle of something.'

OK – that's a complete lie, but I'm trying to sound cool and as if I don't care that the boy I love more than any in the world – other than maybe Jay, but at the moment he's not making it easy for me to even *like* him – is breathing right into my ear.

'Yeah,' says Adam. 'Sorry. I know your brother's come home and that's really cool, right? Thing is – I need to tell you something and I can't really say at school.'

My heart starts to thud and leap at this point. I hate it when people say things like this. Usually it's something really bad, like, 'Your exam has been moved forward to this afternoon,' or, 'You've got your skirt tucked into your knickers,' or, worst of all, 'We think we've found your brother,' which is what happened just before Jay came home and the police had found a body in the canal.

I grip Benjie so hard that he wriggles free and bolts out of my bedroom.

'Spill,' I say. The expression brings unexpected tears to my eyes. It's what Bindi used to say to me whenever I went round to her lovely, warm, crazy home and poured out some problem or another up in her pink bedroom.

'Bindi's not pregnant,' he says. Just like that.

'Oh,' I say. 'How come?'

I'm shivering inside – not sure whether it's shock or relief.

'She thought she was. But she wasn't,' says Adam. 'Something to do with a stomach upset.'

'Oh,' I say again. I can't think of a single thing to say. Not one. You'd think I'd be pleased, wouldn't you? And that I could rush round to Bindi's and reclaim our friendship and pretend that the rubbish last few months didn't happen.

But Adam's news doesn't change the fact that she slept with him when she knew I liked him.

No.

I still feel betrayed.

'Anyway,' says Adam. 'Erm – this feels a bit

70

awkward, yeah? I'd better go. See you at school, Liles.'

Liles.

The nickname makes me shudder. Jay is the only other person to call me that.

Two boys that I loved. One won't speak to me any more. The other went off with my best friend.

Groo.

Some Christmas this is going to be.

* * *

The next day it's Dad's turn to drag me around the shops.

'Dad,' I moan. 'It's going to be hell out there.'

He takes no notice but grips me by the arm and steers me into Mum's favourite clothes shop. He hates shopping even more than I do. Dad looks kind of weird standing in the middle of a department store in his army gear if it's summer or his lion-taming outfit of khaki combats and big fleece with a cap on top if it's winter. His hair is shaved so short it looks more like a shadow than a haircut. And he's about six foot five so he towers over all the well-dressed ladies with their winter coats and strong perfume.

'Just show me what she'd like,' he instructs me, pushing me into a rail of designer dresses and folding his arms. 'And hurry up. I can't take much more of this.'

'Dad, we've only been in here for thirty seconds,' I say, but he's glaring towards the entrance doors now and looking at his watch so I pick out a short black dress in Mum's size and drape it over his arm.

'Right,' says Dad. He marches off to the cash till before I can even say the word 'accessories' so I grab a string of black beads and a sparkly black cuff and rush after him, throwing them on top of the dress just as the assistant is about to put it in a bag.

'OK,' says Dad. He hands over a credit card, punches in a number, grabs the bag off the desk and propels me through the warm crowds of gabbling shoppers and back out into the snowy air.

'Home,' he says. We walk home at about a hundred miles an hour, Dad's long legs striding as if he's chasing an unruly lion.

'Dad!' I pant as he storms ahead. 'I can't keep up. Wait!'

Dad turns around with an impatient look on his face but he waits for me.

We're just trying to walk up the path without

sliding on frozen ridges of ice and snow when Jay comes out of the front door bundled up in a black bomber jacket and with a woolly black hat pulled down over his lank hair and almost over his eyes.

'Where are you off to, son?' says Dad, grabbing him by the arm. 'It's too cold to be out in this weather.'

Jay shakes his arm free of Dad's large hand and makes off down the path and off in the direction of the shops.

We stare after his retreating figure for a moment, gathering snowflakes on our eyelashes and the shoulders of our coats until Dad ushers me inside.

'Don't worry, Lilah,' he says. 'Jay will get back to normal, I promise.'

'When?' I say. I'm aware that my voice is high and sharp but I can't help it. Every time something nice happens, like me and Dad going out together, even if he hates shopping, then Jay ruins it with his moody silence and strange behaviour.

'I don't know,' says Dad. 'But he will.'

I go inside and take a deep sniff of warm cooking smells. Mum has baked home-made mince pies with puff pastry and we gulp down three each with a squirt of cream on the top and a hot chocolate to go with it and we laugh and joke a bit just like a normal family at Christmas time, except all the time we're on edge, expecting the front door to open and the other member of our family to come back again.

Just after three there's a tap at the door and we all jump about nine foot high, me in particular as I've sunk into a chair by the gas fire and am moodily dreaming about Adam Carter and trying not to think about Bindi or to miss her or feel angry.

It's Dr Cunningham.

'Oh, sorry,' says Mum. 'I completely forgot that you were coming!'

She shovels up armloads of old newspapers from the sofa, whips the curtains wide open and takes Dr Cunningham's smart, black, military-style coat.

'I'm afraid that Jay has gone out,' says Mum. 'I would have tried to keep him in if I'd remembered you were due.'

Dr Cunningham gives her a flash of lipsticked smile. I can see Dad eyeing up Dr Cunningham's latest dramatic outfit. She's wearing a high-waisted grey pencil skirt and white blouse with a thick necklace of orange beads and suede ballerina flats in purple with little flowers on the side.

I see Dad glance over to Mum and then back at Dr Cunningham. OK, so Mum's wearing a stained white apron, old black jeans and her cheeks are flushed from cooking all afternoon but I still think she's loads prettier than Dr Cunningham, so I glare at Dad until he realises I've caught him out and then he at least has the good grace to get up and head to the kitchen to make tea.

'Perhaps we can start with you two,' says Dr Cunningham, settling back into our sofa and crossing her shiny legs. 'How's it been over the last few days with Jay back? Do you feel as if you've made any progress?'

I look at Mum and she gives me a small encouraging smile. I know she wants me to tell Dr Cunningham all about the snowman incident. I also know that she does not want me to reveal my true feelings about Jay.

I look from my mother to Dr Cunningham and I realise that if we're going to ever get anywhere with Jay ever again, I need to tell the truth, even if it's not what my family really want to hear.

'Sorry, Mum,' I say. 'But just because we made a snowman doesn't really mean that things are back to normal, does it?'

Mum flushes and turns away, gazing out over the front garden where every single plant and tree is bent heavy with inches of snow.

Dr Cunningham scribbles something into her notebook and then leans forward with her elbows resting on her knees.

'But Lilah, that's great that Jay helped you with something,' she says. 'I'd see that as a breakthrough!'

Mum is nodding so fast that I can almost see two heads.

'That's what I think!' she says. 'We can't expect miracles straight away.'

Dad comes in with a tray of tea. I notice that he's put on aftershave. I also notice that he's put out our best china cups, the ones that usually only make an appearance at funerals or weddings.

Groo.

I don't want Dad to like Dr Cunningham.

I don't like her much myself. Yeah, she's all neat and smiling and saying the right things, but I can see through it. She's just being paid to do her job.

I grab a chocolate digestive because there are only two on the plate and the rest are all dull plain ones and then I look outside and down the street.

'So if it's all going so well, where is he?' I say. 'Where's Jay?'

Dad scowls at me and Mum shakes her head and makes a big thing of standing up and pouring tea, passing it to Dr Cunningham with a shaking hand that makes the cup clank on the saucer.

'Lilah is still very angry,' she says. 'It's one of the reasons we need you here – to help her work through it.'

I roll my eyes and feel my face going tight. As soon as my parents start going on about my anger, it makes me feel even crosser.

'It's not my old anger,' I say. 'It's a new one. 'Cos I thought that when Jay came home I'd be happy again, but he's behaving like an idiot so I can't be.'

Dr Cunningham is nodding away, as if she's my new best friend, and, although it's true that there is a vacancy in that department, I can't think of anything I'd like less, so I clear my throat and fidget about in my seat.

Dr Cunningham drains her tea, looks at her watch and gets up. Dad leaps up too, like she's the queen or something.

Mum stays sitting down.

'That was a rather short session,' she says.

Dr Cunningham gives Mum her professional smile.

'We don't like to always have long sessions,' she says. 'This was just a courtesy call, really. To make sure you're all hanging in there!'

She laughs as though she's been really funny.

None of us join in. I swear I hear Mum mutter, 'Rip-off merchant,' under her breath, but I must have been mistaken. It's Mum who's always banging on about how good counselling is.

She's glancing down the street now, willing Jay to come strolling back in.

I'm still trying to make sense of what Adam told me on the phone yesterday so I don't much care that Dr Cunningham is leaving.

Dad sees her out and Mum just carries on sitting in her chair and staring down the street so I go upstairs and stare at my mobile for a while and then I do the thing I've been wanting to do for over two months and I open up my address book (I've deleted it from my phone) and find the number.

'Nothing to lose,' I mutter to myself.

It's true – I don't have much left to lose. I've lost my favourite boy at school, the brother I used to love and the only thing I might be able to save may just still be worth saving.

I press the little green button.

The ring tone starts up.

I sit on the bed and I wait for her to answer.

CHAPTER TEN

The last time I spoke properly to Bindi, other than our horrid encounter in the chip shop and a pretty difficult phone call, was the day she told me about Adam and the baby.

That was during the summer holidays.

Since then I've gone out of my way to avoid her.

It's been really, really difficult, but because Jay's come home that's kind of taken the focus away from Bindi in my mind for the last few weeks.

As soon as her soft voice answers the phone, all the raw feelings and the anger start to rush up to the top of my head again and for a moment I can't even find the right tone of voice to speak, so I don't.

I just gulp and swallow and stare at the posters on my bedroom wall.

'Hello?' says Bindi again. 'Who is it?'

That makes me sad.

It reminds me of when I used to tease Bindi about not having my name programmed into her phone. She never knew it was me calling until I spoke.

'It's me,' I say, before I can stop myself. 'Lilah. You know – your ex-best-friend, Lilah.'

I figure I should cut the call dead now before I get into a rage. I can feel the red dots starting to flash in front of my eyes and I don't much fancy one of Dad's taming sessions tonight.

I go over to my window and stick my head out and then pull it back in quick.

I forgot it was minus three degrees out there.

'Lilah?' Bindi is saying. 'Why are you calling me? I don't know what we have to talk about.'

'Adam,' I say. I've decided I might as well get this all out in the open.

'Oh right,' says Bindi.

There's a small pause.

'Well, obviously,' I say.

Another pause.

I can picture Bindi wrinkling her nose and frowning with her dark eyebrows, wondering what to say or do next.

'I rang,' I say, 'to see if what Adam told me is true.'

The silence takes on a frostier feel.

'Adam spoke to you?' says Bindi. 'Oh. I didn't know that.'

A small, mean part of me feels pleased when she says that. For a moment I feel as if I might have got a tiny piece of Adam back again.

'Yeah, he did,' I say. 'He told me you're not pregnant. Is that true?'

Bindi sighs.

'Yes,' she says. 'Although I don't really know what business it is of yours.'

I nearly fall off the bed when she says this. Bindi is never rude. Her parents are forever harping on about good manners. It was one of the many things I used to like about her.

'Well,' I say. 'It is kind of my business because I still kind of like Adam.'

There. I've said it – got it out of my system at last.

And actually, it feels pretty good to be honest about it.

I'm fed up with lies. My family has had to deal with enough of them over the past few years.

Bindi gives a small laugh.

'I know you still like him,' she says. 'I see you gawping at him every day at school.'

I feel a flush of familiar heat sweeping up my chest and into my face.

'Maybe you should concentrate on your lessons instead of watching me all the time,' I snap.

I regret that as soon as it comes out of my mouth, but it's too late.

'I don't think we have much more to say, Lilah May,' says Bindi in a firm tone of voice I've never heard her use before.

She's about to hang up but I shout, 'WAIT!'

'What?' she says.

'Do you still like Adam?' I spit out in a garble. 'Cos if you're not having his baby then you don't really have to hang around him any more, do you?'

Bindi laughs again.

'I'm going to have to go,' she says. 'Mum's calling me. Catch you around.'

There's a click and then nothing.

I sit down on the edge of the bed with a heavy thump.

So that phone call left me with no answers and a sour taste in my mouth.

I get up and glance down the street at the

piled-up banks of snow where people have tried to dig themselves out of their drives. The snow is starting to make me feel trapped now. My world is getting smaller.

As I stare down the street thinking about Bindi and Adam, a thin dark figure ambles into sight and lopes up the road towards our house.

It's Jay.

But he's got somebody with him.

A girl – skinny with long, lank, blonde hair and a woolly hat pulled right down almost to her eyes.

And they're – that can't be right! – they're holding hands.

'Mum, Jay's back with a girl!' I yell down the stairs and I hear Mum give a big sigh of relief and run to put the kettle on and she tells Dad to 'act natural', whatever that means, and he shoots up to his study and puts the PC on, even though he's been staring out of the window with Mum for half the afternoon.

Groo.

We're all still acting weird in this house.

When will it ever get back to normal?

And why has Jay got a girl with him?

He comes in, stamping his feet from the cold and with bright red cheeks, and Mum comes out of the kitchen, all casual as if she hasn't even noticed he's been out, and she stares hard at the girl who is dripping melted snow all over the hall carpet. Mum says, 'Oh! I didn't know we were expecting company!' in this bright, false, high voice and the girl stares her straight in the eye and says, 'Oh, sorry,' in a vague, low voice which doesn't sound very sorry at all.

Dad comes back downstairs, drawn by the strange voice in the hall.

'Hello,' is all he says. We're waiting for Jay to explain who the visitor is but instead he brushes past me and goes into the kitchen to make hot drinks.

'Yes, why don't you make your *guest* a drink?' says Mum pointedly, but they're still not rising to it.

I roll my eyes and take a calming breath to avoid my anger bubbling up yet again.

'Look,' I say, barging past Mum and Dad into the kitchen. 'We don't know who this girl is. We are waiting for you to introduce her to us, right?'

Jay shoots me a sullen look and pours hot water into mugs.

'A mate, yeah?' is all he says.

'And does this mate have a name?' says Dad.

He's starting to look a bit annoyed now, too.

'Soz,' says the girl. She's followed Jay into the kitchen and is leaning against the kitchen worktop, slurping coffee like it's the last drink she's ever going to be offered. Benjie has developed a low, threatening growl since she walked into the house. I've never heard him be like this before.

'Soz?' repeats Dad. 'What sort of name is that?'

The girl sniggers.

"Snot my name,' she says. 'It means "sorry". And I'm not his mate. I'm his girlfriend.'

I look at her clothes. She's wearing shapeless, baggy, khaki trousers and a long black jumper that hangs down almost to her knees. Her thin hands are half-covered by ragged green fingerless gloves and she's got her nose pierced just like me, except her face is all pale and spotty and her fair hair doesn't look like it's been washed for about ten years.

I notice something, though. She's pretty, underneath all the spots.

I notice something else. Jay's staring at her as though he's obsessed or something. I haven't seen him look like that for years – since he lived at home and used to stare down at his guitar with a similar expression in his brown eyes.

And there's something else in his eyes. Something I recognise. It makes my heart do little leaps of pain and it makes me realise that Liles, the little sister, has been cut out of the picture.

He used to look at *me* like that – when we were close, when he'd do anything to protect me, when we used to gang up on the Olds, when I was upset about some stupid thing at school and he'd promise to go down and beat up the bullies.

He must love this stranger more than me.

From that moment on, I hate the visitor standing in our kitchen.

* * *

We don't get a lot more information out of the girl, other than that her name is Spud, whatever that means.

'That can't be your real name, surely?' says Dad. He's obsessed with names and words and getting things right.

The girl just gives this irritating little laugh and says, 'Yeah. It is.'

'Rubbish,' says Dad. 'Nobody in their right mind would call a child that.'

The girl laughs again.

'My parents were insane,' she says. 'What can I say?'

Then she and Jay go upstairs to his bedroom, even though Mum has put on her Disapproving Look (tight lips, scowling eyebrows, folded arms) and Dad half-starts to follow them upstairs and then decides against it.

'Spud!' he says, re-filling the kettle and gazing out over the wintry back garden. 'I mean – what kind of name is that for a young girl?'

I'm not really listening. All I can think about is Jay and this girl upstairs in his bedroom and him playing her his Manic Street Preachers music and letting her strum on his guitar and this big engulfing whoosh of pain hits me like a surfer's wave.

'I am going upstairs,' I say. 'And I do not want any dinner.'

Mum and Dad laugh at the same time when I say this.

'You always want dinner,' says Mum. 'OK, I'll leave you a tray for later.'

'If you want,' I say. 'I'm not bothered.'

I'm already hungry.

I go upstairs, lie on my bed and put music on to

drown out the sound of Jay and Spud muttering and playing guitar.

It's ages until Mum brings the tray.

***

When I come down the next day Mum's already up.

'Spud stayed over,' she says, in answer to the question I'm about to ask.

'Where?' I say.

'In the spare room, of course,' says Mum. 'You don't think I'm going to allow her to move into Jay's room, do you?'

I don't tell her that I heard Spud sneaking down the hallway at three in the morning and going into Jay's room. Something about Mum's face this morning warns me that it would not be a good idea to relay this latest bit of unwelcome information.

'How long's she staying?' I say.

Mum turns around from the fridge where she's doing some stress-busting cleaning.

'I don't know,' she says. 'Jay never really speaks to me. So it's a bit hard to find out, really. Maybe you could have a go?'

I get up ready to beat a fast retreat.

'No chance,' I say. 'He's not talking to me either, remember? And I don't want to go anywhere near that girl.'

Mum sighs and slams the fridge shut.

'Well, somebody better find out who she is and why she's here,' she says. 'Looks like we might have another guest for Christmas day at this rate. I don't know how many sprouts to get.'

* * *

Jay and Spud spend the entire day up in Jay's bedroom, but they come down for dinner.

It's kind of a breakthrough because it's the first time Jay has actually come down for a meal without being dragged to the table, but nobody dares say anything. Mum and Dad are so keen to pretend that everything is just like it used to be, but the stupid thing is that they are acting all false and bright and nervy, so nobody is very relaxed.

'Fancy a beer, son?' Dad says as Mum dishes up curry. I mean – Dad never used to offer beer at supper! 'Then I thought maybe we could watch the match? And maybe Lilah and Spud could get to know each other?'

Jay raises his eyebrows at that and just for a moment he catches my eye and there's a little spark of understanding between us, and although he doesn't smile at me I give him a small grin. He waves away Dad's bottle of beer and goes back to pushing chicken lumps around his plate and Spud carries on stuffing potatoes into her mouth with great big smacking noises that are making me feel sick.

'Don't be silly, Mark,' chirps Mum. 'You shouldn't offer Jay a drink when he's . . . well, you know. And he's never been into football. How about a nice game of Scrabble instead? Then we could all do something together!'

I groan and sink down in my chair.

'Where are my parents and why has their place been taken by aliens?' I say.

This time Jay does give a tiny smile down at his lap, fiddling with the black leather bands on his wrist.

Spud sees the smile and stops with her fork half-way to her mouth. She stares at me with her pale blue eyes.

Yeah. I'm right. She hates me as much as I hate her. Some sort of battle has started. A battle for Jay.

The trouble is, I'm not sure I'm going to win it.

Every time Jay looks at Spud he seems in awe of her, as though she rules him or something.

Mum sits down and runs her hands through her spiky blonde hair.

'Sorry, sorry,' she says. 'I'm just so happy to have you home, Jay. You do know that, don't you?'

Jay continues to scowl down at his lap but he gives a very small nod.

'So,' says Dad. 'How do you and Spud know each other, son?'

I don't know why he's asking Jay. Jay never really answers questions any more.

But I haven't reckoned on Spud and her devastating honesty.

'We met on the street,' she says, stabbing at peas with her knife. 'I was sleeping under the Embankment. Jay kind of needed help. So we started hanging out together. I've got a really good dealer. And Jay needs drugs.'

She resumes her pea-eating, as though she's just told us a fairy story rather than a grim tale of heartbreak, drug-taking and poverty, involving my very own brother.

'Dealer?' says Mum. 'What do you mean? Dealing what? Cars?'

'Rachel!' hisses Dad. 'You know what. We'll talk about this later, OK?'

But it's not OK.

Mum's eyes fill up with horrified tears.

'You said he "needs" drugs,' she says. 'Present tense. I thought you'd given up all that stuff, Jay! After two years . . . I just thought. . .'

Jay pushes his chair back and leaves the room.

'You thought wrong,' says Spud. 'Like it's that easy!'

Then she pushes her own chair back but she doesn't follow Jay upstairs. She slams out of the front door instead, leaving Mum in floods of tears and Dad pacing up and down the kitchen like one of his own angry, stressed-out lions. He gets himself a beer and tries to look as if he's enjoying it by making loads of gross lip-smacking noises and sighs of satisfaction but I can tell he's really hacked off.

Mum pours herself a glass of wine and they sit there making a big thing of their drinks so I leave them wallowing in tears, stress and alcohol-induced lunacy and I go upstairs to see what Jay is doing.

His bedroom door is shut as usual but I don't know what's come over me. I feel kind of reckless and a bit wild after my talk with Bindi, and in a way I don't even much care if he tells me to get lost, so I stick my head around the door.

'Can I come in?' I say. 'I need refuge from the Olds.'

Jay's lying on his back on the bed, staring at the ceiling with his headphones in but he doesn't seem to mind me coming in and sitting on the edge of the bed.

After about two minutes he passes me one of the earphones.

I stick it in my ear and the rich, jangly sound of the Manic Street Preachers fills my head.

'It's good,' I say. Jay always loved the Manics.

The thing is – he was listening to them before he disappeared, and he's still listening to them now. Does that mean that nothing's changed?

Is he still planning to leave again?

Why is he still doing drugs?

Does he love Spud more than our family? More than me?

Am I going to lose Jay again, before I've even properly got him back?

All these questions jostle about in my head while the guitar rises and falls and the vocals soar above it, but I know I can't ask Jay any of these things yet.

No.

I can't push it.

I'm sitting on his bed, which is a major breakthrough.

So I lean back against the cold white Artex wall and rest my head against the tiny hard bumps and we listen to the rest of the album in silence and then I take the earpiece out and leave the bedroom because I reckon that Jay wants to be alone again now and I don't really want to be here when Spud gets back.

I can't sleep that night.

Too many things are whirling about in my weary brain.

Jay.

Spud.

Adam.

Bindi.

Mum and Dad.

Drugs.

School.

Anger.

LIFE.

By the time the morning's come I've had about one hour's sleep and I feel like death but I've come to a decision.

The new Lilah is going to stop being angry and start trying to sort things out.

I'm going to be brave and make a visit.

I dress up in my black biker jacket and jeans and wrap a thick stripy scarf around my neck. I tell Mum I'm going out to do some last-minute Christmas shopping and then I walk the fifteen-minute journey that I used to do all the time at home.

I stomp up the familiar path and I push my finger into the bell.

As a figure comes towards me through the frosted glass I take a deep breath and get myself ready.

It's time to start facing things head-on.

CHAPTER ELEVEN

It's been ages since I knocked on Bindi's front door.

There was a time, back when Jay was missing and we were still friends, when I was coming round to this house nearly every day. We'd do our homework together and sit up in her bedroom trying on all her saris and experimenting with her heavy eye make-up and listening to the Asian Network on her sound system.

It was Bindi who got me through the two years after Jay went missing. She was the only one who understood about my anger and how not to push all my wrong buttons.

I've not even been able to talk to her about Jay coming home because we fell out before that actually happened.

So it feels a bit weird and wrong to be standing outside her neat front door and sniffing the savoury smells of meat and onions that always seem to be soaked into the furniture and walls of her house.

I swallow – I haven't had breakfast yet.

This visit seemed more important but now my stomach is trying to eat itself and the smells are only making it worse.

Bindi's mum Reeta is a fabulous cook. She's always got something on the go and I used to get to taste it all too.

Now she's coming towards the front door and I can hear her yelling at Bindi's little brother to turn his music down and there's the usual chaos of noise and smells and clutter as she opens the door and peers round it.

'Yes?' she says in the split second before she realises it's me. Then she hauls open the door as wide as possible and stares at me.

'Lilah!' she says. 'We've been wondering how you are. Such great news about your brother coming home. Come in, come in!'

I wonder for a moment if Bindi has somehow forgotten to tell her mother about our spectacular falling-out but then I realise that Reeta is just being how she's always been – kind, and non-judgemental and keen on people, family, friendships and life.

'It's a bit difficult,' I start. 'I haven't really seen Bindi properly for four months. But I just thought that I should – you know.'

Reeta gestures towards a white sofa with pink furry cushions scattered over it. She pours me a glass of juice and puts a bowl of something that looks like crispy worms in front of me, but they're far more delicious.

'I think you're quite right, Lilah,' she says. 'You two girls were the best of friends. I'm sure whatever has happened between you can be sorted out, yes?'

I sigh.

'You sound like Mum,' I say. My mother has been harping on about my ruined friendship with Bindi ever since it all went wrong.

Reeta smiles and pushes the dish towards me.

'Eat,' she says. 'You look too pale, as usual. I'll go and find Bindi.'

She swishes out of the room, leaving a strong smell of perfume behind her and I try not to eat the bowl of snacks but they're too nice so I end up scoffing loads before she's got a chance to come back again and I'm just gulping down guava juice and wiping my mouth when Bindi slides into the room in her usual way.

'Do you realise you walk sideways?' I say, before I can stop myself. 'Like a crab?'

Bindi smiles. I can't read the smile. It's not in recognition of my feeble joke. It's more like she's decided to be polite because her mother has told her to. Which is probably the case, as Reeta is very big on manners and all the children in her large family have been taught how to look after visitors.

It's a bit different from my own family with their bad tempers, moods and slamming of doors. That's why I used to like coming round here. It stopped me being angry.

Bindi is perching right up on the other end of the sofa. She's almost draped across the arm in an effort not to be too close to me.

'So,' I start, aware that Reeta is bustling about in the kitchen behind us and can hear every word. 'As you said on the phone, you're not pregnant.'

Bindi flinches a bit when I say this.

It does all seem a bit unreal, the thought of Bindi with a baby in her arms.

'No,' she says. 'I had a really bad stomach upset and it stopped me eating. Doctor reckoned that I was too stressed out about exams and everything kind of stopped. It's a bit of a relief, I suppose. Mum went mental when I told her I thought I was pregnant. I'm not ready to have a family of my own yet.'

There's a loud snort from Reeta and the clatter of cutlery and dishes into the sink.

'You can say that again, lady,' she snaps from behind a cloud of steam. 'Sorry, Lilah. But as you can imagine, I was less than pleased that my fifteen-year-old daughter thought she was pregnant by a local schoolboy.'

I expect Bindi to be cross at this but she just gives another mild smile. I suppose she's had all the lectures by now.

'Anyway, now it turns out that she is *not* pregnant after all,' sighs Reeta. 'So we are grateful for that small mercy.'

Reeta sounds quite calm when she says this but I can see her face pulled into a tight scowl as she flings a dishcloth into the sink and just for a moment she looks a bit like Mum looked all the time Jay was missing – kind of grim around the mouth – and I'm guessing that Reeta and Bindi have had some raging arguments over the last couple of months.

She swishes out of the room and leaves us to it.

There's another small silence. Bindi is smiling

down at her lap. I just can't read her expression.

'So should we try and repair things?' I say. This is all so difficult. I feel as if I'm throwing words out into the air and they're just being swallowed up into a big hole, never to be seen again.

Bindi shrugs.

That gets me a bit hot. I know I'm trying not to be so angry now, but I hate it when people shrug. It's rude and doesn't mean anything and I used to do it myself until once I saw myself doing it in the mirror and realised that I looked stupid and ugly.

'Or should we not bother, then?' I continue, glancing down the hall at the front door. I should be at home wrapping up my Christmas presents and not sitting here doing all the hard work. I mean – anyone would think it was *me* who had run off with *her* favourite boy and not the other way round! And I kind of want to go home to Jay and see if we might be able to spend some more time together, anyway.

Bindi gives yet another annoying shrug.

'I don't know,' she says. 'Seems like after you've ignored me for two months at school it would be a bit difficult to pick up where we left off, as if nothing's ever happened.'

I think about this for a moment. The thing is, she's

kind of right. I *did* ignore her at school because I was so hacked off at the thought of her and Adam together behind my back. And she did try a few times to talk to me and I brushed her away. But I can't forget what she did to make me act like that in the first place.

'Well, I came here to try and sort things out,' I say, standing up and brushing sesame crumbs off my jeans. 'But you don't want to, so I'll go home and try and mend things with my brother instead.'

Bindi nods. For a moment she has the grace to look sorry.

'How is he?' she whispers. We used to share everything – every feeling we had. In the old days I could have bitched about Spud and how she's cast some awful spell over my Jay. Now I don't even want to tell her stuff about Jay. It seems kind of private and belonging to my family and nothing to do with her any longer.

'Getting there,' I say. I head off towards the door but something is still bugging me and I've got to ask her.

'By the way,' I say, just as I reach the front door, with Bindi hovering behind me as if she can't wait for me to go. 'If you're not having a baby with Adam, I guess you won't be interested in going out with him now. Will you?'

Bindi laughs. It's not her usual laugh. I turn around until I'm looking her straight in the eye.

'You'd like that, Lilah May, wouldn't you?' she says, still in her soft voice but with something new and hard behind the eyes. 'Because you like getting your own way, and if you don't you throw a hissy fit and get into a temper.'

I'm so shocked at this that I back up against the open door and bang my back hard on the catch.

I turn round and am about to run down her path so she can't see my tears but she hasn't quite finished. A firm hand grips my arm and swivels me round again. This time her face is really close to mine.

'Yes, I still like Adam,' she says. 'And he still likes me. And we're going to carry on going out. So I'm afraid that your little plan hasn't worked out. Goodbye.'

Then she pushes me out of her house and slams the front door.

I stand there staring at the green-painted wood for a moment and then I set off home with tears pouring down my cheeks.

So I've lost my best friend and I've lost Adam and I've kind of still lost Jay because he hasn't really come back to us properly yet.

I walk home in a kind of trance in the slush and the snow and a fresh fall of flakes dusts my hair and makes my face cold but I don't really notice.

I don't think things could get much worse.

Could they?

✳ ✳ ✳

In fact, they could.

As I reach the end of our street and turn into it, I realise that Jay's standing on the opposite side by the postbox and he's not alone.

I duck back out of sight and drop down behind a wall.

There's another boy with him, or more of a young man, really – about twenty or so.

Jay's got his head hidden beneath his hood and he's stamping his feet against the cold.

The other guy is fiddling about in his pockets. He glances about and then he passes a small white packet into Jay's closed fist and mutters something before sloping off out of our street and leaving Jay to walk home alone.

I come back out from my wall and run to catch him up.

'Hey,' I pant. 'Where've you been?'

Jay does a shrug that looks a bit like Bindi's but I ignore it.

'Shopping?' I say. I'm not going to let on that I saw him. I want him to tell me about it unprompted.

Jay gives a small snort that may or may not be a laugh, or a cough, or a noise of disgust.

'Yeah, little sis,' he says. 'Shopping. Goodwill to all men and that!'

Then he speeds up and gets home first, with me panting and puffing behind.

Spud is leaning out of Jay's bedroom window and when she sees him coming she yells down, 'About time! Get up here!'

He goes straight up to his bedroom and shuts the door.

I know what he's doing up there and it's as if the past two years haven't happened and I've rewound back to the time just before he went missing and I burst into his room and first caught him doing it.

I go into my own room and lie on the bed in a haze of misery. Clumps of snow drip off my boots and melt all over the duvet but I don't care.

I can hear Mum and Dad having some sort of argument downstairs in the kitchen and there's no smell of cooking so it looks like we're not getting lunch.

'*Groo*,' I mutter, but it doesn't even touch how I'm feeling today. I must make up some new Lilah-isms. My old ones are rubbish.

Then my throat feels scratchy and I sneeze.

Oh great. I've caught some hideous lurgy just in time for the holidays.

'Happy Christmas, Lilah,' I mutter at my grey reflection in the mirror.

I stagger downstairs to join my warring parents.

✳ ✳ ✳

There's something I've noticed about Spud.

Jay's always staring at her with this weird look on his face – part awe, part love and part fear.

He gets worried when she's not around and paces up and down looking out of the window until her tiny frame lopes into sight.

But Spud doesn't look at Jay that way.

In fact, she spends most of her time glaring, either at me, or at Mum and Dad.

She even made like she was going to kick Benjie once but I threw myself between them and glared at *her* so hard that she's never tried to go near him since.

Spud doesn't seem to notice Jay and he looks really hurt by that. The only time she talks to him is when she's muttering about where her next fix is coming from and then Mum and Dad try to break it up fast by changing the conversation to something stupid like takeaways or television.

It's as if Jay thinks that Spud is his girlfriend but she's got other ideas.

She's bugging me so much that I do a wicked thing.

I go through her stuff.

She hasn't got much of it so it doesn't take long.

There's a horrid smelly khaki bag that she wears slung over her body in a diagonal line, presumably so that nobody can grab it off her and steal her drugs.

One day I wait until she's in the bathroom having one of Mum's suggested baths and I creep into the spare room and pick up the smelly bag.

Ugh.

It feels *damp*.

I hold my breath and rummage about inside with one hand, trying not to breathe in the odour of cigarettes and stale water and whatever else she's got in there and I turf out old bus tickets and tiny stubs of squashed lipstick and a selection of needles and bits of old tin foil and then I find her battered mobile phone.

There's the sound of water running in the bathroom. She'll be a while.

I click the phone on and press the little envelope that opens the text messages.

There's a stream of them in the inbox. All from the same person. Some bloke with the lovely name of 'Rat'.

The very latest message has got today's date on it. It says:

Miss U. Leave that loser and come back to London. Rx.

I feel my anger boil right up from my feet to my chest in record time.

I fling the phone back into the horrid bag and go off to my room.

I need to think.

***

That afternoon Mum and Dad decide to summon us to a 'Family Conference.'

Groo.

We haven't been called to one of those since before Jay went missing. In the old days the conferences used to be about silly things, like, 'We need to put a rota in place so that you do your fair share of helping Mum keep the house tidy,' or, 'Your great-aunt Hilda has died and we want to discuss what to do with her caravan in Prestatyn.' Kind of stupid things, but at the time they seemed very important and the four of us would sit round the table for ages making a mixture of silly and sensible suggestions until the conference fell apart and we'd all end up laughing.

I'm not sure there's going to be too much laughing at this one.

Mum's got big circles under her eyes again and Dad's only just got back from an emergency at Morley Zoo so he's already fraught and rushed and fed up and he somehow looks too big for our small kitchen in his Morley Zoo sweatshirt and combats.

I'm in a foul mood after my visit to Bindi. I keep seeing her cruel eyes and her smug little smile and then the odd vision of lovely Adam Carter floats past it all and I get a pang in my stomach.

I really miss Adam.

We used to have loads of fun.

But it seems like I've lost him, Bindi *and* Jay all at the same time.

Mum puts five mugs of hot chocolate on the kitchen

and produces a bag of marshmallows.

I rip the bag open and scatter the mini-pillows all over my drink with enthusiasm. Then I look up and see both Jay and Spud staring at me like I'm some sad freak in a zoo. This is rich, because I'm not the one wearing a stupid woolly bobble-hat indoors. Spud never takes off her hat, I've noticed.

I wonder if she's gone bald from taking drugs? I wonder if that's possible? I'm just chewing that one over and spooning marshmallows onto my tongue when Dad raps on the table with a spoon and nearly gives me a heart attack.

'Right,' he says. 'Family conference time.'

I see Jay look at the kitchen door.

Dad looks at the same time. Then he gets up, produces a key I've never seen before in my life, and *locks* the kitchen door!

'I didn't know we had a key for the kitchen door,' murmurs Mum.

Jay looks over at the window but Dad's one step ahead of everything today.

'Double-locked,' he says. 'Fat chance, son.'

Jay glowers down at his lap and fiddles with his dirty fingernails.

Spud just laughs. I think she's enjoying this, from

110

the way she's staring round at each of us in turn and smiling.

It's not a pretty smile. It's a challenging one. I can really imagine Spud toughing it out on the street.

Not like Jay. He's more fragile.

It's beginning to make sense to me now. I can see that my big brother's been led astray by Spud and others like her. He might pretend to be all hard, but I can see that somewhere underneath there might just be a bit of the old, soft Jay left behind.

How do we get it out, though?

'OK,' Dad's saying. 'Well, you know we're so glad to have you back, son?'

Jay gives a brief nod and shrug and a noise that sounds like, 'hrmphhh.'

'Right,' says Dad. 'The thing is, we hadn't reckoned on having another, erm, person here for Christmas this year. Had we, Rachel?'

'No,' whispers Mum. She looks very awkward and refuses to glance in Spud's direction. 'I don't know how much food to buy.'

'That's not the pressing issue here, Rachel,' snaps Dad. 'We have plenty of food. But we need to work out how the five of us are going to get through Christmas and what we can do to help Jay and Spud. Right?'

Mum nods and sniffs into a big crumpled handkerchief with an 'M' embroidered onto the edge of it.

'So, I'm presuming that you do want to stay for Christmas day, Spud?' says Dad. I notice that he stumbles a bit over the word 'Spud'.

Spud licks a moustache of hot chocolate from her lips and gives an abrasive snort.

'Haven't got any better offers!' she says. 'S'pose it's either that or going back to my box on the streets.'

I feel the familiar rush of heat coming up from my legs towards my head and I grip the table.

Dad comes over to stand behind me. He puts his hands on my shoulders and I can feel the warmth coming through from his big fingers.

'Don't rise to it, Lilah,' he says in a quiet voice. 'Remember that other people don't have the advantages you have in life.'

'Like being taught manners,' I say, before I can stop myself.

Jay swears under his breath.

Dad groans and Mum buries her face in her hands.

'Don't you start, Lilah,' says Dad. 'I mean it. This is not helping one little bit.'

I take another slow deep breath and try to avoid

looking at Spud with her horrible little smirk and jiggling arms and legs. I've noticed she can never keep still for more than about one second. She's always fiddling about with something or buzzing with some horrible fake energy.

'Spud is Jay's girlfriend,' continues Dad. 'And although we are not in any way pleased about the idea of drugs coming into this house, we are prepared to let her stay here for a few days with various conditions put in place.'

Uh-oh. I know what Dad's conditions are like – harsh.

Jay knows as well, judging by his sour expression and the way he too is jigging his legs up and down.

'Ooh, conditions!' says Spud in her horrid drawling voice. 'Goody!'

I look at her pale, pretty face and her thin chin and glaring blue eyes and for a moment I wonder how good it would feel to get up and smack her, but then I think of all the work Dad has done on taming me this year, so I try to do what he's suggested and not rise to it. At least, not yet.

'So,' Dad says. 'The first condition is that you do not bring any more drugs at all into my house – either of you. Got it?'

Spud laughs and looks at Jay, but to give him credit he's flushing red.

'I've stopped,' he mutters. 'Honestly. I have.'

I stare at him in disbelief. Yeah, right.

'That's as may be,' says Dad. 'But you will both see Dr Cunningham before Christmas when she comes to the house and I will ask her to sort out some appropriate treatment for you both. Agreed?'

To my surprise, Jay nods.

But Spud's got up now.

'Open the door,' she says. 'I need to get out and get my fix. This is doing my head in.'

Dad draws himself up to his full height. I almost expect him to roar like Lazarus or Samson, his big cats at the zoo.

'Well in that case,' he says, 'you are not welcome back in my house. You walk out now, you're not coming back in. End of.'

Dad is terrifying when he's like this, but Spud is still sneering at him and rattling at the door handle.

'I'd sit down again if I were you,' I say. It's the first time I've directly addressed a sentence to Spud since she got here.

Her eyes light up like they're on fire.

'I wondered when little sis would start interfering,'

she says. 'It's all your fault that Jay ran away in the first place, isn't it? If you hadn't dobbed him in to your parents he'd never have had to start sleeping rough!'

She's standing by my chair now. I can smell her horrible odour of sweat and stale tobacco and something else, something I don't even want to think about.

I stand up so that I can look straight into her eyes.

'I'm not scared of you,' I say. 'You're not part of this family and you never will be. Jay only likes you because you can get him drugs. And you're just using him so that you can have a roof over your head here. I know all about your other boyfriend.'

I hadn't planned to use my new bit of information so soon, but she's pushed me to it.

Her smile fades a bit at that and I see in a flash that she's come to rely on Jay needing her and she's never really thought about what might happen if that need goes away.

'You little bitch,' she says. 'Jay was right about you.'

I look over at Jay. He's got tears in his eyes but he looks up at me and shakes his head and in that moment I see that Spud is a troublemaker and a liar and that Jay hasn't been bad-mouthing me at all.

Dad has decided to intervene before a fight breaks out. He unlocks the kitchen door and holds it open for Spud to leave.

'You don't come back here unless you're prepared to seek medical help,' he reminds her.

Spud spits.

It misses Dad and lands on the floor.

'That's nice,' I say, before I can stop myself.

She pushes past me – hard. Then slams out of the house.

Jay goes upstairs, soundless as a tiny mouse.

His bedroom door shuts and there's no sound of music.

Mum pushes past me in tears and screams, 'A happy sodding Christmas this is!' as she goes upstairs.

Dad sighs and shakes his head at me.

'Why do you always have to lose it, Lilah?' he says. 'We could have tried to sort this all out. But no – you have to interfere. I'm ashamed of you.'

Then he too goes away, leaving me sitting at the kitchen table with my life in tatters around me.

CHAPTER TWELVE

School breaks up for Christmas and although Adam catches my eye and gives me a half-smile, we don't get to talk to one another at all. It's difficult with Bindi following him about and giving me hard stares, so I give up even trying and I sit through the school Christmas lunch of watery turkey slices and freezing cold tangerines without speaking one word to anybody.

I feel about as lonely as I've ever felt.

* * *

On the fifth day of my so-called holidays I'm lying up on my bed with Benjie squashing my chest, and I'm trying not to cry for the millionth time and wishing

117

that I could ring Adam and hear his lovely gravelly voice. I've taken out my anger diary and looked at it but I can't seem to find the right words to express everything I'm feeling so I put it back under my pillow and carry on lying there. Then I hear the doorbell ring and the sound of Dr Cunningham's voice, so Dad's obviously stuck to his word about getting her over and I hear her say, 'Well, it *is* Christmas eve,' in a rather pointed way and I sigh and bury my head back in the pillow until Mum comes back and taps on my door and says, 'Lilah? We need you to come down, love.'

It's the first time she's called me 'love', even though she said she forgave me the day after our argument, so I creep downstairs and before I go into the lounge to see Dr Cunningham, Mum gives me a brief hug and wipes my eyes with her big embroidered handkerchief and I say, 'Yuk!' which makes her smile, and we go in together.

To my total surprise, Jay's sitting there . . . with Spud.

'Oh,' I say, before I can stop myself. 'You're back.'

Spud snorts in her sarcastic way but Jay says, 'Yeah. I went and got her,' which surprises me even more, so I just say, 'Oh,' again and go and sit near to the gas fire because I'm freezing.

Dr Cunningham is wearing jeans and a jumper, which is quite unusual. She sees me looking and says, 'I'm supposed to be on leave, but your father did say it was urgent.'

Mum pours Dr Cunningham a cup of tea with her trembling hand and makes to pour one for Spud but Spud says, 'Tea? That's an old person's drink!' so instead Mum creeps back to her chair and folds into it without another word.

'So,' starts Dr Cunningham. 'I gather that you'd like some help with drug dependency?'

Jay and Spud go all fidgety and start staring out of the window when she says this so Dad takes over.

'Yes, please,' he says. 'What's the procedure?'

'Well,' says Dr Cunningham. 'I can't provide that sort of help myself. There are specialist counsellors who will be able to directly address the issues your son and his, erm, friend, are struggling with. And I can refer you to a methadone clinic where Jay will get help breaking his addiction step by step, if that sounds all right?'

'My name's Spud,' says Spud. 'And I'm not his "friend". I'm his girlfriend.'

Jay coughs and I give a loud snort.

119

Dr Cunningham gives Spud a penetrating glare over the top of pink-rimmed specs for a moment.

'Quite,' is all she says, but it's enough to have me start at last to like Dr Cunningham. She looks a lot more human in her jeans and jumper with her hair in a messy ponytail than she does when she comes round all dolled up in suits and flowery blouses.

'Biscuit?' I say, jumping up to offer Dr Cunningham the last chocolate digestive. I only do this because Spud's been eyeing it up for the last five minutes.

'Thank you, Lilah,' says Dr Cunningham. 'I am actually on a carb-free diet – but as it's Christmas!'

She takes a delicate bite of the biscuit and I enjoy the cross look on Spud's spotty face.

'Lovely,' says the doctor. Then she fills in about three hundred forms, gets Mum and Dad to sign them and stands up, brushing digestive crumbs off her dark-blue designer jeans.

'I can carry on doing your family therapy sessions after Christmas as per usual,' she says as she's leaving, 'if you still feel the need for them?'

Mum and Dad and I all look at one another. In that brief flash of silence I take in Mum's wrinkles and puffy eyes and the faint shade of grey that's starting to take over Dad's number one haircut and I realise that I feel a lot older than I actually am. With one voice we say, 'Yes,' and Dr Cunningham looks quite pleased and wishes us all a happy Christmas before roaring off in her posh blue people-carrier.

'So,' Dad says when she's gone. 'That's good, Jay, isn't it? You'll be finally able to get your life back on track, once and for all.'

Jay kind of mutters a response to this but Spud's looking furious.

'I need a fix,' she says.

Dad smiles.

'By all means,' he says, holding open the lounge door for her. 'But you won't be spending Christmas day with this family, in that case. Cold out on the streets in the snow, is it?'

I stare at Dad with admiration. He's good. He's very good.

Dad pushes the address of the methadone clinic into Jay's hand.

'Do us all a favour, son,' he says. 'Get down there now. Go on. Go.'

And to my surprise, Jay looks at the address, gets up, grabs Spud by the hand and disappears out of the front door.

'Do you think – you don't think. . .' begins Mum, but Dad silences her.

'Just wait and see, Rachel,' he says. 'Have a bit of trust in our son.'

Mum looks doubtful but she takes Dad's hand and I leave them and go upstairs to wrap the rest of my presents.

CHAPTER THIRTEEN

It's Christmas day.

Last Christmas day was pretty bad and the one before that was even worse, because it was the first one since Jay had gone missing and we had to do this false jolly thing where the three of us played stupid games and stuffed ourselves with turkey and then Mum went off to cry over the washing-up and Dad shut himself upstairs with his computer or read his lion magazines in stony silence, and we all wished that the hideous day could be over.

I had this picture in my mind of what life in this house would be like if Jay ever came home again. He'd be smiling and fleshed out again and look more like he used to – brown curly hair, red cheeks and big grin. Mum would be back to doing her clown job again and she'd be smiling with happiness at her family being complete. And Dad would be full-time at Morley Zoo, helping the lionesses give birth and seeing to all the sick and newborn animals and coming home with his eyes shining to tell me all about what Shyama and Lazarus, the big lions, were up to.

Some hope.

Christmas day in the May household doesn't get off to the best start ever.

Daughter (that's me) gets up with stinking cold and staggers downstairs clutching aching head and begging for painkillers and tissues.

Mother forgets to put the turkey on until nearly lunchtime and, because it's too big, it takes five hours to cook, so we end up having omelettes and roast potatoes for Christmas lunch.

Father is called out to a zoo emergency and spends the morning away from the house instead of opening his Christmas presents.

And Spud's back. She did go to the clinic with Jay and they've been given methadone and put on a programme that they've got to stick to if they want to pack in the drugs. But she's still a complete and utter nightmare and has been rude to everybody in the usual way.

And she and Jay stayed up half the night listening to the Manics and when I heard this a chill gripped my heart and I thought, *Maybe nothing has changed.*

So whereas once I'd have rung Bindi and had a good old moan about all this, I now have to sit up in my bedroom staring at the black top I chose for my present and not really having the heart even to try it on.

I really, really want to ring Adam and wish him a happy Christmas, but that would be a rubbish idea. He's with Bindi. I heard her loud and clear.

In the end I kidnap Benjie from the kitchen and force him to lie on the bed with me while I have a good cry into his furry paws and he looks at me with big, sad eyes.

'You're my only friend, Benj,' I sniff in between sobs and he rolls onto his back and exposes lots of white fluffy tummy so I play with him for a while and feel a bit better.

Dad comes back at lunchtime and we all sit around the table with the Christmas omelette and Mum says, 'I wish I'd known I was cooking omelettes – I could at least have got some mushrooms,' and we all stare down at our plates trying not to say anything that hurts her feelings but thinking of the white wrinkled turkey still half-frozen in the oven.

'Never mind,' says Dad in the false jolly voice that he's been using for the past few weeks. 'There are more important things to celebrate this year, Rachel.'

'Yeah, and I'm a veggie,' says Spud. 'Can't eat turkey and all that shit. So omelette is kind of cool.'

It's the first vaguely nice thing she's said so Mum gives a forced smile and says, 'More spuds, Spud?' which makes Jay smile down at his lap.

Dad raises a glass of Ribena because Mum forgot to buy any wine and all the shops are shut.

'To Jay being home again,' he says. We clink glasses with Jay. He's hardly touched any food and is sitting slumped in his chair gazing down at his lap as usual.

'To Jay,' whispers Mum. She looks at her son with eyes full of worry and sadness. I guess she didn't think that it would be like this when he finally came home, either.

'And we've got presents!' announces Dad. He's obviously rushed to a petrol station and bought something for Spud at short notice.

'Oh,' she says, ripping off the paper. For a moment she flounders for what to say. Then she says, 'Cheers.

I haven't had a present for nearly four years,' and then she opens the box of Black Magic chocolates and starts to stuff them into her gob.

Dad ferrets about underneath the table and brings up a parcel, which he tosses to Jay.

Jay doesn't say anything. He rips off the paper and holds up a Manics T-shirt.

'Cheers,' he says. There's the faintest glimmer of a smile, but it's a pathetic cousin of the grin he'd have once given Dad for a gift like that.

Mum passes him her presents.

'Thought you could do with some new gear,' she says. 'You've grown!'

Jay gives her a faint smile but after opening the present he puts the pile of clothes untouched on the kitchen table.

'OK, then,' says Dad, all the time in this forced, cheerful voice that doesn't sound much like his own. 'Time to unleash plan B. Step outside, son.'

Jay rolls his eyes at this and exchanges a sarcastic look with Spud, but he gets to his feet and follows Dad outside. Mum and I grab our coats and follow them onto the front drive.

There's a strange car parked where Dad's zoo van usually sits.

'So?' says Dad. 'We reckoned that you were old enough and ugly enough to start lessons. How about it?'

My mouth is hanging open.

OK, the car isn't exactly brand new and it's very small, but it's a car. A whole car. So Jay comes home after two years when everybody has been worried sick about him, and he gets a reward like this.

'Not fair,' I mutter at my boots, but Dad hears me and his smile fades.

'Now just a moment, Lilah,' he says. 'There are conditions attached to Jay having this car. I was about to get to that.'

I shuffle about in the snow and scowl at my feet.

'One, he has to be totally drug-free before I will even consider paying for lessons,' says Dad.

Spud gives a snort at that. She's followed us out and is aiming lame kicks at one of the tyres on the red car until a glare from Dad puts a stop to that.

'Two, he gets himself some sort of job and pays for the tax and insurance himself,' says Dad.

'And three?' I say, because it's obvious that there's a third condition by the way that Dad's still facing Jay with his serious face on.

'Three is that in three year's time, Jay gives *you* lessons, Lilah,' says Dad.

That takes the wind out of my sails.

'Oh,' I say. 'Oh – OK, then.'

I give Dad a small smile.

'So what do you think, son?' says Dad.

Jay has hardly looked at the car even though Spud's been sizing it up and walking around it, no doubt imagining her horrible puny frame sprawled across the passenger seat.

'It's OK,' mutters Jay. Then he heads back inside without another word.

I watch Mum's own smile fade back into lines and wrinkles of worry and I start feeling that hideous familiar feeling rising up from my feet to my knees and then towards my chest. If it gets to my chest I'm in trouble.

Uh-oh. It's gone way past my chest and to my head.

Dad knows the signs after trying to tame me for the past few months.

He places his hands on my shoulders from behind.

'Lilah, don't,' he says. 'It's Christmas day. No anger today, huh? Let's just be glad that Jay is home at last. Can you do that for me?'

I look upwards into Dad's eyes. I can see up his nose from this angle. Gross.

'No,' I say, surprising even myself. 'No, I can't. I've had enough.'

Dad shepherds us all back into the warm kitchen and forces me to sit down.

Mum goes over to the freezer.

'Christmas pudding will be ready later,' she says. 'So how about some ice cream?'

Her voice has gone all high and false again.

Great.

Jay's scraping his chair back to make his usual escape back to his dank, dark bedroom but I'm quicker than he is.

'No you don't,' I say. I'm blocking the kitchen door so that he can't make a run for it.

'Get lost,' he mutters. 'Move.'

But I don't move.

'I've had it with you,' I say. 'You've ruined the last two years and now you're ruining Christmas for everybody again. Mum and Dad are trying to be kind and they've just bought you a *car*, a whole *car*, when they've only bought me a stupid top, and you're just throwing it back in their faces. Why? What's wrong with you? Oh yes, I know. I know what's wrong with

130

you, don't I? I saw you with that man on the street. You said you were giving up, but you're still doing it, aren't you?'

Mum claps her hand over her mouth when I say this. Dad shakes his head.

Jay is always pale as the moon these days but when I say this he gets even paler and starts to sweat.

'You're talking crap,' he mumbles, trying to push underneath my arms but I'm not having it. I seem to have taken on some super-human strength, as though my arms were made of steel and bolted to the frame of the kitchen door.

Mum and Dad have kind of melted into the background. I see Dad try to come towards me, but Mum stops him and whispers, 'This has been a long time coming, Mark. Let her get it out,' which surprises me because Mum hates shouting and argument.

'No, I'm not,' I say to Jay. My voice is quite low and calm now. Another surprise. Yeah, I'm angry, but in a different way. It's not the usual exploding type – more a kind of steely-determined and honest type.

'I'm not letting you put me in this position again,' I say. I blow my nose because my cold's getting worse. My heart is pounding. 'That's what got us all into this mess in the first place, remember?'

Jay is shaking his head.

'You're nuts,' he says. 'Get out of my way, loser.'

'No,' I say, slamming my arm down again and staring him straight in the face. 'You're using drugs again. You used to use drugs, right? And I told Mum and Dad, which was the hardest thing I ever had to do and I was only twelve. You told me not to tell them and I did and then you went missing. And it was all my fault and I've had two years of *shit* and beating myself up for that and you don't *know* how hard it's been for me here, and for Mum and Dad!'

Mum is crying at the kitchen table and Dad looks ashen.

Even Spud has stopped smiling and is looking at me in a different way from usual. I swear she looks a bit . . . scared.

Jay laughs.

'Get lost,' he says. 'Like it's been a picnic for me living on the streets.'

I see great curtains of scarlet when he says that. It seems that my new pledge not to get angry is about to be broken.

'That was your *choice*!' I yell. 'We didn't *have* a choice. We just had to live through over two years of

132

hell because of your stupid, selfish behaviour.'

Dad gets up at that and starts to come towards me but Mum pulls him back again.

'Lilah's right,' she says. 'In fact, I think it needs to be said and I think Dr Cunningham would agree that we should get all this out in the open. You put us through hell, son. She's right.'

Then Mum's face crumples and Dad gets a tissue out of his safari jacket and passes it to her.

Jay's stopped trying to escape now and is staring at me with something in his eyes I've not seen before. It takes me a moment to see what it is.

Fear.

That's what it is.

I'm the little sister, but I've frightened my big brother.

I can't stop, though. I've got too much to say.

'Because of you,' I say, 'my whole life has been ruined. I've lost my favourite boy at school because he couldn't cope with my anger. I've lost my best friend because she's going out with him. I've failed all my exams and had about a million detentions. And that's all because of *you!*'

With that last word I aim a vicious kick at the door just by Jay's leg. It's either the door or the leg,

I reckon, so I have to choose the door.

Jay's legs buckle under him and he grabs at the kitchen table and then slides back into his chair and buries his face in his hands.

I think he's laughing because his shoulders are going up and down and this makes me so mad that I'm about to haul him out of his chair and yell at him some more but then I realise that he's not laughing.

He's crying.

Jay's crying.

I haven't seen him cry since he was a little boy.

'OK, Lilah, enough now,' says Dad. He goes over and sits with Jay, holding his hand.

Mum blows her nose and then gets up to fill the kettle.

'Some Christmas day,' she whispers. 'I just wanted to have all my family together again, and happy. But I don't feel as if I'm ever going to be happy again.'

Jay's sobs get louder and he looks up through a haze of tears and runny eyeliner and says, 'M . . . Mum?' and then he gets up and kind of falls against her and she puts her arms around him and they both cry some more.

Spud goes upstairs and shuts herself in Jay's bedroom.

I leave my family in the kitchen and go up to lie on the bed.

I feel spent and empty but as though something heavy has at last got off my chest and left me alone.

I stay up there the rest of the day drinking Night Nurse and coughing. I go to bed without speaking to anyone. Mum puts a few slices of turkey and some roast potatoes and Brussels sprouts outside my bedroom door and I'm starving hungry so I eat them in the middle of the night. She's forgotten the cutlery and it's kind of difficult eating gravy and meat in the dark but I stuff it all in, anyway.

I don't cry any more, though. I've cried myself out this week. There aren't any tears left to cry and if I cry it makes my cold feel worse.

But I've left things bad with Jay.

So – what's going to happen tomorrow?

CHAPTER FOURTEEN

When I wake up the next day my head is still thick with cold.

I fling back the curtains and squint against the bright, cold sky. There are still several inches of snow lying around but it's beginning to thaw out on the trees and water drips onto the snow on our back lawn and makes black holes. Robins hop in and out of them, looking for worms.

'Thank God Christmas is over,' I mutter to my grey reflection in the mirror. Then I tug a comb through my black messy hair and wrap myself up in my thick pink dressing gown.

'Morning!' says Mum, as if nothing happened yesterday. 'How's the cold?'

'Rubbish,' I say, making myself a honey and lemon drink and blowing my sore, raw nose.

'Oh dear,' she says. 'You're not having a very good holiday, are you? Sit down. I'll make you a nice breakfast. I've got some bacon left over from the turkey.'

I smile at her because I can see she's had a rough night too. There are purple rings under her eyes and her hair is all squashed on one side and sticking up on the other.

'Where's Dad?' I say. I heard his van roar off early.

'Samson has attacked another male lion,' she says. 'Usual old thing.'

I nod and roll my eyes. We're used to Dad's emergencies at the zoo.

'And Jay?' I say. 'Where's he?'

'Gone out to get something from somewhere,' she says. 'He wouldn't say what. But he did kind of show an interest in the car this morning. Asked Dad for the key and just sat inside it listening to music for a while. Not sure where he's gone now.'

My heart sinks.

'Drugs,' I say. 'It's got to be drugs. Why else would he go out?'

Mum sighs.

'I really hope you're wrong, Lilah,' she says. 'But I've booked him an appointment with a drugs counsellor next week and I will be dragging him there by the hair if necessary and making sure he continues to go to the methadone clinic.'

'Good,' is all I say, but I smile. I'm relieved that she's not angry with me after my major outburst yesterday.

Mum can't get the bacon off the top of the turkey so we end up eating cold turkey for breakfast in companionable silence and then the door slams and Jay bursts into the kitchen, shaking snow off his black jacket and shivering from the cold.

'Do you want a drink?' Mum asks. He nods and she makes coffee for all of us.

'Where's Spud?' I say. I haven't seen her yet today.

'Gone,' says Jay. 'She's not going to do the clinic. She's gone back up to London to meet this Rat guy.'

'Oh no,' says Mum. 'That's really sad. I hope you're not going to follow her example, Jay.'

Jay shakes his head.

'Nope,' he says. 'I've had enough of her. She can suit herself.'

Mum exchanges a small smile with me over the top of Jay's dark head.

'So what did you go out for?' I say. I try not to sound suspicious and like a nagging adult but that's exactly what my voice comes out like.

'Nothing,' says Jay. 'Don't worry about it.'

'Hmm,' I say. 'That's a bit difficult, really, isn't it? When I saw you doing a *drugs deal* in the street.'

Jay gives me a look. It's hard to read it but his eyes are brighter and there's a faint splash of colour in his pale cheeks. At least he's speaking to me. And the atmosphere feels different from yesterday – like a rubber band has stretched to breaking point and then snapped and fallen into a heap on the ground. The air feels softer.

'Can we just drop the talking-about-drugs thing, yeah?' he says.

I pull a face.

'I'm going to try to stop, all right?' he says. 'I can't make any firm promises, though. It's not going to be easy.'

'Are you going to learn to drive?' I say. 'Can I come out with you?'

Jay gives the smallest of smiles.

'One thing at a time,' he says. 'Jeez, Liles. Drop the pressure, OK?'

I risk giving him a smile and after a moment he

139

gives me another tiny smile back.

'Upstairs,' he says. 'Come on.'

I look at Mum and she shrugs her shoulders so I follow my brother up the stairs into his bedroom and he throws himself onto the bed and then chucks an envelope at me.

'Happy Christmas, Liles,' he says.

I'm so surprised that I can't speak for a moment.

'It's not drugs, is it?' I say, before I can stop myself.

Jay buries his head in the pillow with an exasperated roar.

'Will you shut up about drugs?' he says. 'Like I'd start trying to get *you* into them! OK – I made a mistake. I'll be trying not to do it again. And Mum's forcing me to go to some counsellor and I've said I will. So get off my case, right?'

He's not actually smiling, but there's a bit of life in his voice for once. He's looking a bit like the old Jay, except thinner, and a young man now, not a boy.

I have this spark of joy building up inside me but I don't want him to see that so I rip open the envelope and two tickets fall out.

'The Manics are playing at Wembley,' says Jay. 'Want to come?'

I stare down at the tickets in my lap and big fat

tears plop onto them so Jay rescues them just in time and then comes and sits close to me. We're not touching, because we've got a long way to go until that ever happens again, but I can feel the warmth of him next to me, and now that he's had a few baths I can smell his real Jay smell, like the one he had when I was little. It smells of jumper and shampoo and hair gel.

I take a deep breath. There are things I've been wondering for over two years and pictures I've had in my head and now I want to know whether they were right or not.

'What was it really like, living rough?' I venture. 'How did you get food and stuff?'

Jay grimaces.

'Loads of ways,' he says. 'Spud was very good at conning people out of money and stealing stuff. Now that she's gone, I wouldn't have the money to buy drugs, even if I wanted to. Some nights we got soup and stuff handed out by charities and that. I used to beg, sometimes. All those posh people coming out of the theatres, you know?'

I nod. I went to London once with Mum and Dad and we saw a play in a big theatre and then walked back to the Tube across a bridge where there were loads of dirty-looking people sleeping in bags and boxes underneath. Dad told me I shouldn't ever give money to these people because they only spend it on drugs.

'Where did you sleep when it was really cold?' I say, because it looks like Jay's going to answer my questions now.

'Churches, sometimes,' says Jay. 'Broke into people's sheds. Some nights we got lucky and got a bed in the Salvation Army place. And we got six months in a squat once until the owner came back and booted us out.'

I shudder. I can't imagine not having a roof over my head. I don't even like it when Mum and Dad force me to go on camping holidays and sleep on rough wet ground under a canvas tent. And even though Mum and Dad sometimes drive me demented, I know they'll always make sure there's a bed for me here, even when I'm old.

'But what about after that?' I say. 'How did you keep warm?'

Jay gives a snort.

'Didn't,' he says. 'Spent a lot of nights kipping on park benches or just walking up and down to try and keep blood flowing, you know?'

I nod, even though I don't know. The thought of Jay all small and sad and sleeping on a park bench has haunted my dreams for two years but I never actually thought that he really *did* end up doing that.

'Oh,' I say in a low voice. I can feel tears coming up again into my eyes. I spent the entire two years that Jay was missing being unable to cry, and now I can't seem to stop.

When I've finished my embarrassing sob-fest I blow my blocked nose. I have one more question to ask Jay, though. I'm not sure he's going to be able to answer it.

'Jay,' I say. 'Why did you come home?'

Jay fiddles about with his guitar strings and makes a few twanging noises. He doesn't look me in the eye but his voice goes a bit huskier when he answers.

"Cos it's home,' he says.

I sense it isn't the whole reason. I reckon Jay came home because he needs our help but he's not going to admit that because of silly boy pride.

'Yeah, of course,' I say. I apply a rim of Vaseline to my cracked, sore nostrils and laugh at my reflection in Jay's bedroom mirror.

'Oh *groo*,' I say. 'No wonder Adam Carter doesn't like me. What a sight!'

Jay's picked up one of his many other shiny red guitars and is strumming the strings with his dark hair falling over his face, but he looks up when I mention Adam.

'Why do you think he doesn't like you?' he says.

I laugh.

'Erm, because he slept with my best mate, d'oh!' I say. Visions of Adam and Bindi flash in front of my unwelcoming eyes.

'Maybe he slept with your best friend because she was easier to work out than you,' he says.

'Well – yes,' I agree. 'And that's because I was angry all the time. Because of – you know what.'

'Me,' says Jay. 'Sorry. I've been such an arsehole, haven't I?'

There's not really any way that I can deny this so I just smile and nod a bit and he looks sad and guilty so I grab the guitar off him and play the chords to 'Mull of Kintyre', which is the only thing I can play, and he groans at my pathetic attempt and we stay up there for another hour.

It's great, but all the time his words about Adam echo in my head and I think, *What if he's right? What if Adam only went out with Bindi because he couldn't cope with me? What if I stopped being angry and was nice to him instead? Or does he really love Bindi?*

'I'll be back,' I say to Jay. 'I just want to make a phone call.'

I leave him playing along to the Manics. There's a faraway look in his eyes and his hands have started to shake and I realise that Jay and I have still got a long way to go before things can ever be 'normal' again (whatever that means).

I shut myself in the bedroom and pick up my mobile phone.

✳ ✳ ✳

Adam answers in his lovely gruff voice.

'Lilah? This is a surprise.'

I nod, which is stupid because he can't see me, and then I decide I'm going to come right out with it.

'I know it's probably too late,' I say. 'But I want to say I'm sorry. For being angry all the time. I'm not now. Things are better with Jay. So I just wanted to kind of say that, OK?'

'Yeah, OK,' says Adam. 'You are a bit of a nightmare, Lilah May. But that's why I like you. Never a dull moment, right?'

I laugh.

'So if you're still going out with Bindi,' I say. 'I hope the two of you will be really happy.'

To my surprise I kind of mean that, even though I still get a pang inside to think of the two of them together. But getting Jay back is the best thing ever so I figure I can't be too greedy and want *everything*.

Adam gives an embarrassed sort of laugh.

'Erm, I'm not going out with Bindi,' he says. 'I never was. It was one day, one mistake. I was mixed up about you, yeah?'

I sit down because my legs have turned to custard.

'She seems to think that you still like her,' I say. 'And she certainly still likes you.'

Adam sighs.

'She's been texting me a lot and following me about,' he says. 'Thing is – she might like me, but I don't really like her that way. Well – not as much as I like somebody else.'

My hearts falls into my biker boots and gets a sound kicking when he says that. Oh great. He's found another girlfriend. Perhaps Bindi and I can set up some sort of ex-girlfriends-of-Adam-Carter club.

'Oh, that's nice,' I say. My voice comes out like a baby lamb, all wobbly and broken and faint.

'I hope she's pretty.'

Adam laughs again.

'Yeah, she's pretty,' he says. 'She's also a bit of a nightmare. Like I just told you. But I still really want to ask her out again.'

I clutch at my pillow with one hand. Nightmare? *Nightmare*? But – that's what he just called me . . . oh!

I lie back on the bed and wave my legs in the air and make silent punches of victory and grin for England. Thank God my mobile doesn't make video calls.

'So how about it?' says Adam. 'Cinema? Tonight? My shout?'

'Yes,' I say in a small whisper. 'Yes please.'

Then I hang up the phone and bite my pillow with joy.

CHAPTER FIFTEEN

I'm, like, so made up that I've got another chance with Adam Carter, the hottest boy on the planet.

But there's something bugging me.

Big time.

My life doesn't seem quite complete, still.

There's one thing missing.

I want my best friend back. But will she ever want to be friends with me again?

* * *

I've been thinking about Bindi a lot.

I've realised now why I miss her so much.

It's because Christmas used to be a time when I'd get together with my best mate and we'd swap silly presents and stuff ourselves with food and then go down to the January sales together with my Christmas money and her allowance and come staggering back with loads of plastic bags before trying it all on up in my bedroom.

It's because whenever there was a boy that I liked, Bindi would be the first person I'd tell and we'd spend hours discussing what I should say to him and what I should wear and how I'd react if he ever asked me out.

It's because even before I became a teenager, Bindi had come up to me one day at school with her shy smile and asked me where I'd got my gold ear-studs from and I'd taken the tiny heart shapes out of my earlobes so she could hold them. By the time that the bell rung for break we'd somehow become firm friends.

It's because when I was really down after Jay went missing, Bindi spent hours just sitting next to me and letting me ramble on about everything, or nothing, and even when I was quiet and miserable and didn't want to talk, she'd send me little cards in the post with hearts and flowers on, and sometimes a bangle or a bookmark would fall out of the envelope and lift my heart a bit, even when I never thought I could smile much again.

It's because Jay really liked Bindi, even though some of my friends made him roll his eyes and disappear up into his bedroom, and he sometimes let her play on his guitar and even taught her a couple of chords before that dreadful day when he left home and didn't come back.

It's because I really used to like going round to Bindi's house and spending time with her siblings and her kind, dramatic parents with all their arm-waving and tasty cooking and loud exclamations. They sort of made me feel like I was one of the family, even though didn't always feel part of my own.

It's because Mum and Dad always used to put their arguments aside and become more good-tempered whenever Bindi came round to do homework with me, and Mum was always telling me that boyfriends can come and boyfriends can go but true friends should last a lifetime, or at least a pretty long time.

She's been saying that to me all my life.

And the thing is – I know she's right.

✳ ✳ ✳

I give it loads of thought and I discuss it with Mum,

and as usual she tells me just to be honest and to put my true feelings in a letter, if I feel that I can't go round to Bindi's house and deal with it face-to-face. I'm a bit scared she'll be horrible to me again, even though I know that Bindi really isn't a horrid person at all.

So I sit up in my room with Benjie lying across my feet and I power up my computer and just write it all out in a big rush. This is what I write:

Dear Bindi,

Please don't rip this up. It's me, Lilah – the girl who used to be your best friend. And, deep down, I kind of hope that I still am. Or can be.

I know why you were angry with me. I should have stuck by you and been there for you to talk to when you thought you were pregnant. I should have noticed that you were lonely at home and had loads of pressure from your Olds. And instead I did a typical Lilah and I huffed off and got myself in a temper about it. It's just that I liked Adam so much. I love him. You have probably heard that we're giving it another go. I really hope that you can forgive me for this, but you'll remember that, back in the days when we were mates, you encouraged me to ask him out, so I think you know just how much I really do like him and I hope you can understand.

You were a brilliant friend to me when Jay first went missing and I couldn't have got through it all without you. So I'd kind of like to be friends again if you can forgive me for abandoning you.

If you can't, that's OK, but I'll be sad. We were best friends for so many years and I miss you, Bind.

That's it.

Love,

Lilah.

I print the letter off and then I decide to show it to Mum.

'What do you think?' I say.

I elbow Jay out of the way. He's trying to read over my shoulder.

'Girl stuff!' I say. He rolls his eyes and walks out into the snowy garden to roll a cigarette. Mum and Dad have allowed him to keep one filthy habit so long as he gives up all the rest.

'Lilah, it's lovely!' says Mum. 'I'm proud of you for being so honest.'

She wipes her eyes and heads off to yoga with my letter sealed up and ready to post.

Then I spend the next days in agony, waiting to see if there is any reply.

There is.

It takes five days for it to come and I've chewed my nails down to the quick and taken Benjie on about a million walks around the block to try and calm myself down but one morning when the mail plops onto our mat I see her neat black writing on an envelope and I nearly die of stress.

'I don't want breakfast!' I yell as I pound upstairs with the letter clutched to my heart.

I throw myself on the bed, offer a silent prayer up to the Great God of Friendship and rip it open.

I smile.

Bindi is still not very up to scratch with computers, even though we use them for loads of things at school.

She's written her letter by hand in a tight black scrawl. I have to scowl at the words and hold the paper near and far to try and work out what it says. This is what she's written:

Dear Lilah

Thanks for your letter. Sorry I can't type this one back to you but I can't remember what my password is on the home computer. Useless with technology, as ever!

Anyway, it was brave of you to write. I was really rude

last time you came round and I hate being rude so I'm sorry about how I behaved. It was a really difficult time – Mum had only just forgiven me for the pregnancy scare, Adam was being kind to me but I knew that he still liked you.

I'm not stupid, Lilah. I could always see him looking at you. I just wanted to believe that he liked me better and that was stupid and childish, so I'm sorry about that too. Things are better now at home.

I'd like to say that we could be best mates again but I think it's going to take a bit of time. So could we just be mates, to start off with, and see how things go from there?

Love,

Bindi.

I hug the letter to my chest and take a long, deep, calming sigh of relief.

'It's good,' I say to Benjie.

He pushes his wet nose into my hand.

'I think I might one day get my best mate back,' I say.

Then I take the letter downstairs to show Mum.

CHAPTER SIXTEEN

I think I'm going to only write in this diary once a month or so, now. I don't feel as if I'm going to be angry all that much any more, or at least, only as much as normal people are.

You see, I've got my brother back again and my favourite boy at school, so I can't really waste too much time being foul-tempered and miserable any longer.

Mum's just come upstairs and told me she's hoping to go back to clowning full-time, which is brilliant, and Dad's giving up his Friday nights in the pub and is going to spend time with Jay instead. So the May family are back to normal again – or, at least, as normal as we ever were in *the first place – if you don't count Jay's drug counselling and our continuing sessions with Dr Cunningham.*

And I think – I HOPE – that soon I'll be able to start working on my friendship with Bindi again. It will be different this time round, but that doesn't mean it can't be good, does it?

✳ ✳ ✳

I'm dreaming.

I'm eleven years old and I'm on a canal boat with Mum, Dad and Jay.

Mum and Dad have gone off for one of their evening pub meals and Jay and I are lying on top of the boat on our stomachs with our legs crossed up in the air behind us and a can of shandy that Dad's left us for a treat.

Jay's got his earphones on and is nodding his head up and down to the music.

His hair is brown and curly and his face is glowing with health. I can see all the tiny freckles on his cheekbones and scattered across his nose.

Just for a moment the sun goes in and a dark cloud heavy with rain passes over the canal and causes me to shiver and look around for my jumper.

'Here,' says Jay, chucking it on top of me. 'Don't get cold, Liles.'

I look into his brown eyes and for a moment I'm scared.

'Jay,' I say. 'Jay. You won't ever leave me, will you? You'll always be my big brother?'

Jay turns and stares into my eyes, so close that I can see the flecks of hazel and green in his pupils.

He grins and reaches out to pull my plaits.

'Yeah,' he says. 'Yeah. I'll always be here.'

The canal water laps at the edge of the boat and warm sun streams down on our backs.

In my sleep, the last little dregs of anger melt clean away.

Vanessa Curtis
spent the best part of a decade playing
in very loud rock bands which is why
she can't remember much about her twenties.
However, these days her brother plays in a band,
so she can leave the wild partying to him and
concentrate on writing books for children instead.
She lives near Chichester Harbour with her
husband and cat and still likes to crank up Planet
Rock to full volume when there's nobody in.
Vanessa is the award-winning author
of *Zelah Green* and *Zelah Green:*
One More Little Problem
and *The Taming of Lilah May*.

Vist Vanessa's website at
www.vanessacurtis.com

If you enjoyed

you can visit www.taminglilahmay.co.uk
for more news and information.

By the award-winning author of
Zelah Green, Queen of Clean.

THE TAMING OF LILAH MAY
Vanessa Curtis

I'm Lilah May and I'm ANGRY. So angry
that I'm about to be excluded from school,
my parents can't control me, and only one
person in the world understands me. And
that's my best friend Bindi.

I haven't always been this way. It all
started with my brother Jay. And what no
one realises is that it's all my fault.

Why did you want to write these books about Lilah May?

I thought it would be interesting to explore what might happen to a close, loving family if one of their members went missing unexpectedly and how a teenage girl would cope with intense feelings of anger and guilt as a result of that disappearance. I also thought it might add some humour to have Lilah's father be a modern-day lion tamer and her mother to be a rather miserable clown!

Where do your ideas come from?

A lot of my ideas come from watching documentaries on television or reading articles in newspapers. Of course not all of the ideas will make great books – there has to be something unusual or different about an idea to make me truly want to explore it further.

There are a lot of musical references in these books. Are you influenced by music? What's your favourite music/band?

I trained at music college to be a pianist before I became a writer but dropped out to join a couple of pop/rock bands which is why my twenties passed in a bit of a blur(!). I still write all my books to a chosen soundtrack on the computer – in fact I find it difficult to write fiction without listening to music! I used to be in a pop band and then a heavy metal band, but my favourite groups are an eclectic mix – so I like groups like Green Day and The Kaiser Chiefs, but also some old stuff from the 1980s like AC/DC and Whitesnake – I'm a bit of a metal-head, in fact, and listen to Planet Rock to make the cleaning less boring. In complete contrast to that I also enjoy listening to baroque, renaissance and classical music!

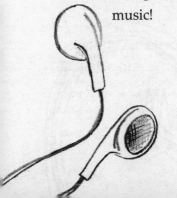

Did you always want to be a writer?

I'm not sure I always wanted to BE a writer, but I have always written. At school I used to do well at English Language and enjoy writing essays and stories. I was published in the school magazine a few times. I started really wanting to do writing as a job when I was in my teens and used to get paid to write pieces of journalism for magazines.

Were you influenced by what you read when you were younger?

To a certain extent, although the books that kids enjoy today are very different from the ones I enjoyed when I was younger – they had a sort of innocence which is less obvious today. Nowadays it's more acceptable to explore various challenging issues in books for 10+ and in fact kids seem to really want to read about 'gritty reality' – which is handy, because that's the sort of stuff I enjoy writing.

Do you have any advice to your readers who might want to become writers?

Read everything you can get your hands on! Reading is essential if you want to develop a sense of how to invent likeable, believable characters and come up with gripping storylines. I read a lot of books written for young teens.

What's the most difficult thing about writing for young adults?

Knowing that every single word has to count. Young adults are very honest readers and if they don't like something, they'll tell you!

What are the good and bad things about being a writer?

There aren't too many bad things, luckily. There's a certain amount of having to deal with rejection, having to rewrite parts of your books again and also an awful lot of Waiting. Most writers become experts at Waiting! But the good things, when they're going well, are REALLY good. Imagine coming up with some characters, thinking of what might happen to them and then

being able to put this all down on paper and see it published in a book which then sits on the shelf of your local bookshelf. That's a true thrill. And one of the other really good things is reading what kids think about your books and sometimes getting to meet your readers in person to discuss what they like or even don't like about your books. That's the best thing about having written a book.

THE END